Introduction to Write by The Sea in Folkestone 2020

I had dreamt about starting a writing group in my home town of Folkestone for a couple of years. There were many strands to my vision; putting pen to paper is only one small part of the writing process that leads to creating a lasting memory.

I wanted to encourage anyone to write but also give them the tools and foresight to see that others have succeeded. To enable this, I arrange a visitor once a month to come and talk to the group about their journey and experiences. This could be authors, illustrators, photographers, script writers - anything to do with the writing and the making of a book.

I wanted a safe place for our meetings; the environment had to be calm and welcoming to create the perfect place for sharing thoughts and ideas. Our member numbers have grown since we started in October 2018, as has the group, even during corona we have kept in touch, to encourage and help each other. This anthology was completed during lockdown by email, messenger and zoom. The group really came together at a time when the world was changing rapidly due to the pandemic.

This is our first of hopefully many publications, so sit back and take a tour round Folkestone and enjoy reading about the ghostly goings on.

If you would like to join our friendly group, please drop me a message.

Karen Marwood

www.karensworld-writer.co.uk

karensworld.writer@yahoo.com

First published in Great Britain in 2020 by Wealden Strand Publishers @wealdenstrand

Photography by Mark Brophy, cover photograph by A L Marchant

Paper Edition : ISBN 978-1-9161801-4-7

eBook Edition : ISBN 978-1-9161801-3-0

Foreword – by Charlie Gallagher.

Folkestone is an Art School
And a centre of creative excellence, a bohemian haven for the artists and poets, the writers and all things creators. It thinks differently; its very buildings are poets after all:

Weather is a third to place and time – anyone?

And yet, this isn't true. Folkestone is a place. It cannot write or draw or sculpt or rhyme. It's an assortment of buildings - and when the buildings run out? Either the changing face of the ocean or the rugged terrain of the North Downs takes over. It is a small place then, penned in by nature at its most raw.

And yet Folkestone **is** an Art School.
And it is the people that make it so.

I have fourteen published novels; drama my choice of delivery, fear and hope the emotions I want my art to elicit, and each of those novels feature Folkestone. Sometimes as the backdrop, sometimes just a place that blurs through a car window while a main scene takes place – sometimes it is the main protagonist itself. There is something about this place that inspires me, that rawness of the nature on show perhaps, the contrast of the slate grey sea with the vivid green hills – there is no place like it.

But it is the people that make it so.

A little while ago, Karen Marwood created a writing group as a way of sharing her passion, reaching out to discover if this place we all love is really the lightning rod of creativity it presents itself to be. What she got was Folkestone showing us what it has, turning out its creatives – all ages, all shapes, all sizes, all genres. All with undoubted ability.

What follows is a collection of their work, presented by Karen. As varied as the sights that surround us, and all with this place as the starting point. And that should be enough on its own to make you want to dive straight in.

Another sight in the town, another building displaying its art:

Heaven is a place where nothing ever happens.

This collection of our finest is a place where anything can happen.

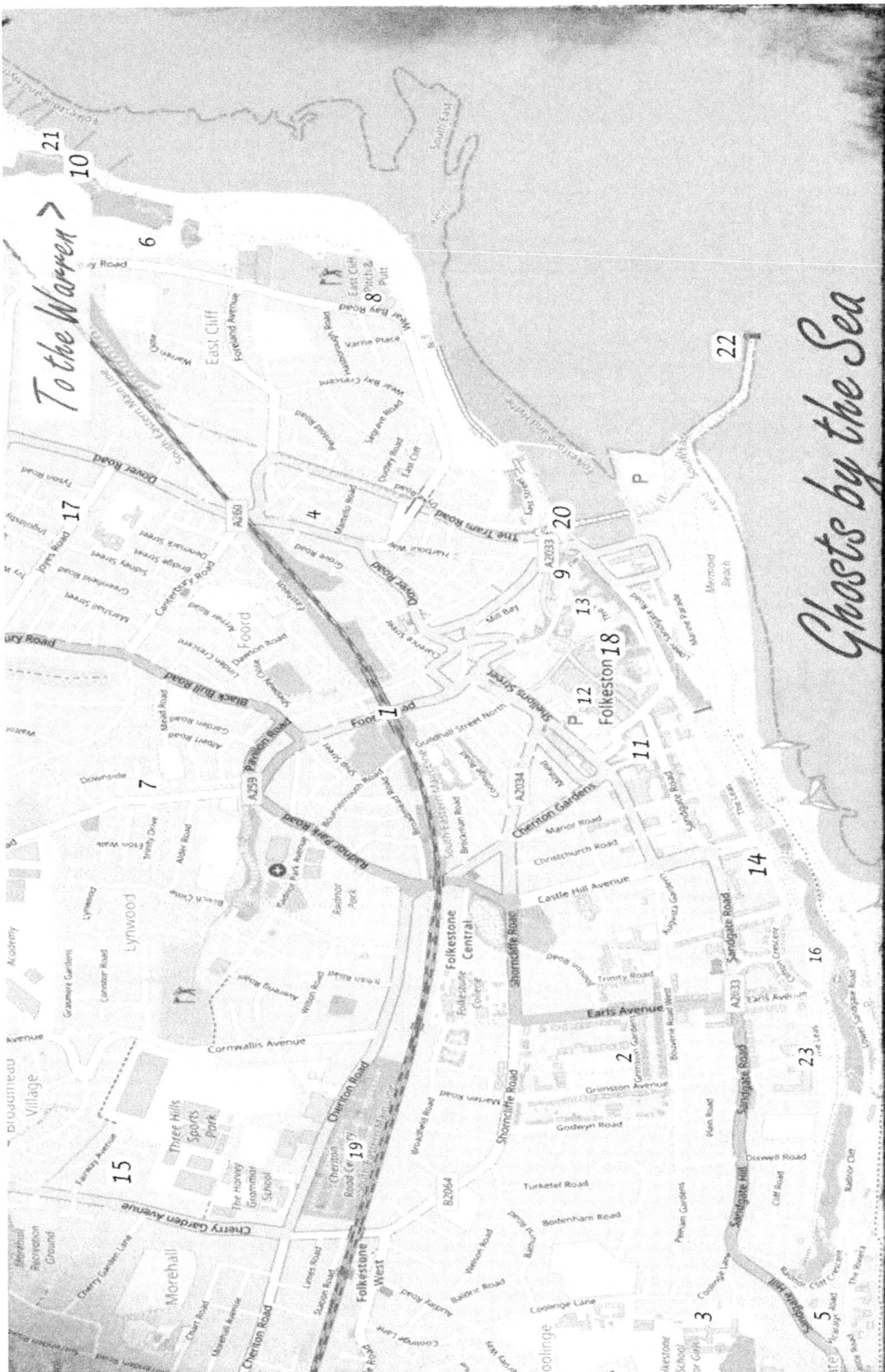
Ghosts by the Sea
To the Warren >
1
2
3
4
5
6
7
8
9
10
11
12
13
14
15
16
17
18
19
20
21
22
23
Folkestone
Foord
East Cliff
Lynwood
Morehall
Coolinge
Folkestone Central
Folkestone West
Three Hills Sports Park
Radnor Park
Mermaid Beach
Dover Road
Canterbury Road
Black Bull Road
Pavilion Road
Radnor Park Road
Cheriton Road
Cheriton Gardens
Castle Hill Avenue
Shorncliffe Road
Earls Avenue
Sandgate Road
Sandgate Hill
Cherry Garden Avenue
Cornwallis Avenue
Foord Road
Tontine Street
The Tram Road
Wear Bay Road
Christchurch Road
Manor Road
Bouverie Road West
Grimston Avenue
Grimston Gardens
Godwyn Road
Turketel Road
Bodenham Road
Coolinge Lane
Jointon Road
Trinity Road
Guildhall Street North
Marine Parade
Lower Sandgate Road
The Leas
Radnor Cliff
Dixwell Road
Broadfield Road
Marten Road
Joyes Road
Tyson Road
Dawson Road
The Harvey Grammar School
Folkestone School for Girls
A260
A259
A2033
A2034
B2064

1

A Ghost in a Viaduct

by Carol Grimes

Folkestone Viaduct. A Victorian citadel looming tall below the ridge of hills that enfold the seaside town on the Kent coast. I have always admired Victorian industrial architecture. The grand buildings that heralded the new age of steam and travel. Railways and trains, mighty engines and the herculean bridges that span the rivers, estuaries and deep valleys. This viaduct was built in 1843 crossing the harbour with thirteen soaring arches and is the world's highest brick viaduct, Grade II Listed status given in 1975.

One cold evening in Autumn, the winter clocks had turned an hour backwards a few days before, the sun dipped and it was suddenly dusk, soon to be dark and I was standing underneath the Viaduct in Folkestone. Alone. I have always been afraid of the hours of darkness. I shivered.

Shssssss - *"Hello."* A reedy whisper, barely audible?

A chilly wind whipped around my hatless head rustling a cluster of autumn leaves beneath my feet. I don't like a chill wind. I do like facts. So here are some facts. Buildings were being made in red clay bricks in southern Turkey and Jericho around 7000BC.

"Hello?"

I am a little bit rustled myself. Am I hearing voices? More facts. Bricks, useful and beautiful. Industrial workplaces. Hearth and home, town halls, hospitals, factories, railway stations and magnificent arches all made from the humble brick.

"Hello?"

On the edges of my eye I sense a faint presence, almost transparent, like the fragile wings of a grey moth and gossamer thin. My eyes are not that good these days. I call myself "One eyed Lil."

"I am up here."

Where?

"Inside the bricks."

Bricks! Inside the bricks? There are millions of bricks.

"Yesses, I am aware of that. I was one of the "butty" gang building the viaduct. Me and my work horse. Some of the clay came over from the rubbish dump. Look up!"

Am I actually having a conversation with myself? I resume my fact checking. The rubbish dump is the elegant Kingsnorth Gardens now. The Viaduct, tall and mighty, bestriding Countryside, Town, City and Hamlet, wherever the railway needed to travel... people moving ....

"Look up, into the arch, look up."

.... constantly moving. Where are they all going to?

"Look up!"

Yes right, but there are so many arches.

"This one."

Who *are* you? What are you? I'm scared now. I'm going home.

"Lucky you."

Where the *Hell* are you?

"In Hell. How did you know where I am?"

I whirled around, my head was spinning inside a kaleidoscope of bricks and time. An electrical current fizzed through my veins and my bones felt like ice...

"My grave has been inside this Viaduct since 1843. One hundred and seventy-six long and lonely years."

I gasped. Oh, I am very sorry.

(But where are the apparitions? The ethereal robes of dusty grey?)

"I have been up here with steam trains thundering over my head, shaking my bones. What teeth I had still in my mouth, have been jiggered out of my jaw."

(The sour smell of the long ago deceased?)

'A Spitfire flew through one of these Arches. Mad! Would have taken my head off, if I still had a head."

Spitfires? Steam trains?

'High speed trains. A hundred and eighty-six miles per hour? Who needs to travel at that speed? Hurry, hurry. The world is in such a hurry.'

(Where are the swirling mists, the cries of the forlorn and forgotten dead?)

"So fast, all too fast."

Come on ... Gird your loins woman. Back to the facts. In January 1844, the railway viaduct was completed, a hundred years before my birth.

'Good view up here. I can see for miles. I can see France. I can hear the guns."

He seems to dwell in the past and the present, now, then, tomorrow. hours, days, years, all blurred as one. An anarchic take on time, travelling across the years with no rhyme or reason. A maze with no exit, no entrance, no order, meandering and slip sliding through centuries.

"I keep a watch over the Harbour: ships travelling away to exotic places. Then, the troops off to Flanders. Ferries to France. Goods shipping through the English Channel, around the Bay of Biscay. The Cape of Good Hope... out to The British Empire... all built ... on the backs... of people like me. They can go to blazes."

The voice seems to trail away, sensations of movement, a melancholy shifting shadow? The arches are growing in stature, reaching up into the darkening sky. Scraping and scaring the clouds. British Empire?

"Me? I'm stuck here. Bricked up for eternity, and more. If the whole viaduct tumbles, what happens to me? My dust, my remains?"

War? First World War? I am not about to look for invisible voices. Run more like it. No, *that* could be dangerous and paranoid. Walk calmly and purposefully away. *He*, for it is a male voice, is still talking.

"Nineteen arches you know, the tallest in the World. William Cubitt built it. His brother was a part of the development. Where there is money? Family connections. Wealth and control. Keep it in the family. Nothing has changed. Unlucky for some, unlucky for me!'

I am talking to a ghostly spirit. Dwelling in the supernatural? Moving slowly away from underneath the arches, quaking in my shoes.

(Facts, not phantoms, pull yourself together.)

"Yes, we all shoved, shifted, shunted and chivvied, pushed and pulled. Millions of bricks you know? Hard and heavy work.'

I feel my eyes misting...tears for fears?

"My horse died. They couldn't get us out. Truth is, we were abandoned, bricked up for ever more. Left behind and forgotten."

(Where are the sounds of the clinking and dragging of old rusty chains? The chains of restraint, the chains of the working class?)

"I don't know where I'm going. Hell's fire or heavenly clouds of choirs and angels! Or a nothingness, a void? What year are we in?"

2019.

"Strewth. I have been looking for God."

Did you find him?

"No. But I need to be saved or forgiven. And I am dust. A mere puff could blow me into infinity."

The more I look for the owner of the voice, the more *he* is not there. The cloak of invisibility shrouds his very existence. Does he even exist? If he does, how do we know that he is a he, a man, a boy, a human?

"Murdered Mary is a'wandering in her white dress, around the Royal Pavilion, now...the Burstin .... and the Anglia, she's going down.'

His voice is becoming fainter, as if he is talking to himself.

(Where is the ectoplasm and the opaque grey mists?)

"So many dead are down there among the rocks in Old Davey's Locker. Lying on the sea bed, bones picked clean."

Poor man. Lying in his grave inside a Viaduct for all those long and lonely years, with nobody to talk to.

(Where are the ghostly howls and wails? The moans of the desperate and the cries of despair?)

"Whit Sunday, fire. The Pier is burning... 1943, war is still waging. I heard the bombs, I felt the tremors, I heard the screams. They built a tunnel underneath the Channel. That was an upheaval. Disturbing the watery graves of those who were drowned in war or disaster."

(Where is the smell and the stench of death?)

"Goodbye, don't forget...me..."

A grey cloud slides sinuously across a waxing silver moon. Something moves, as if penetrating mortal flesh and bone. My flesh and bone.

"Shhhhh... "Goodbye."

There *is* no *body* waving goodbye.

" Shh GOOOOOOD.......hiss..."

All I hear is my breath and the beating of my own heart. Where has he gone? He has vanished. Retreated into older times? Or future times? Spirited away into an unknown abyss on dark spirals of smoke. Do the dead mourn a lack of ritual? Was there a wife, children? Was he a boy or a man? I will mourn him and his horse. The bleakness of his grave, no body for a burial, no tears, no hymns sung, no scattering of earth into a coffin. He didn't rest in peace.

A flock of birds fly above my head as I turn my feet for home and the moon, and a scattering of stars peep out in between scudding clouds of grey as I walk away towards Bouverie Road West.

2

Grimston Gardens

by Jane Cottle

Lockdown was difficult for everyone, Lisa knew that, but she felt she had an excuse for feeling it was worse for her.

Here she was on her own in a new flat and a new town where she wanted to be but didn't know anyone yet. Just three days ago she had completed on the purchase and moved in. She knew that there was always a possibility of a lockdown coming so she had pushed hard to bring the completion date forward. She had managed it in the nick of time even if she was a bit stuck on her own now.

Colleagues were surprised when she told them she was moving to Folkestone, but she really liked the feel of the place. It had a sort of faded grandeur and a sense of history. She had been an avid listener to "Home Front" on radio four and felt that she wanted to live in the place that was so significant in the events of the Great War.

She found this beautiful place in Grimston Gardens online. What had originally been quite a grand residence had been completely updated and sympathetically converted into two self-contained apartments. She booked a viewing for the ground floor garden flat and it was even better than she expected. The road was tree lined and surrounded a garden that was beautiful even in the winter. Her apartment had the original front door which was very elegant, and the front windows had shutters which gave it a slightly continental look. Inside it had been beautifully refurbished with heritage paint colours that enhanced the original fireplaces and other features. The living room had French windows that looked out onto a small but quite private garden that caught the sun even on that early January day. She offered the full asking price, which was accepted, and moved in on the 19th March.

On 23rd March the country was put into lockdown and she was going to be living through it in Grimston Gardens.

She face-timed her mum to show her round.

"Sorry mum. I know you were really looking forward to coming down to help me move in."

"Don't worry darling, it can't be helped. At least you're in now and are not stuck in limbo betwixt and between. I can come down when all this is over, and you're settled in. They say it will only be for three weeks. I feel you're much safer down there than you were in London."

"Well it certainly feels safer here. The top floor people haven't moved in yet and now they won't be able to for a while. I'm so glad I got the broadband sorted. I've already checked in with the office, although strictly speaking I'm still on leave."

"Can I see this wonderful garden?"

"Ok. Here are the French windows, I'll open them and try and show you. Ooh it's a bit chilly, good job you can't feel that through the phone. It's quite bare at the moment just with new turf but the trees round the edges are quite mature and give it a nice enclosed feeling. I want to get some more colour in here, I hope I'll be able to get some bedding plants."

"What's that behind you? That black patch in the middle of the lawn?"

"Oh that. It looks like there has been a bonfire or something. It's a shame really that it was done after the new turf was put down. I'm not too worried, I am sure it will soon grass over, I can always get some seed if necessary. Anyway, I am going back inside now as I'm getting cold."

It was exciting cooking in her new kitchen. The microwave had been her best friend in her old kitchenette but here she felt more inspired as she stood at the granite worktop chopping vegetables and looking out over the darkening garden. She had thought of getting a blind for this window but now she was not so sure. It wasn't overlooked and she had nothing to hide. As the light faded away, she could see her reflection in the glass almost as if she was looking in a mirror. She startled slightly as she thought she glimpsed a movement behind her and turned quickly still holding the knife in her hand. Of course, there was nothing there. She opened the window and realised that the movement she had seen was just the branch of a tree outside. The way it had merged with her reflection had confused her for a moment. She took a deep breath and continued with preparing the meal. Maybe she would get a blind after all. She opened the window and smelt a breath of smoke. She supposed that someone further down the road was having a bonfire, or maybe someone had a wood stove. It seemed so quiet outside. She hadn't realised how noisy London had been until she moved here.

Tomorrow she would go out and take her permitted exercise. There should be enough time for her to walk to The Leas and back. She still couldn't get it into her head that the sea was just walking distance away now.

It was unseasonably warm as she walked up Grimston Avenue the next morning and there were no people about. The air smelt fresh and sweet. It was a green smell with just a small tang of salt. She stopped for a moment and breathed in deeply. It was hard to believe that the country was at war with a deadly virus when all around her the signs of spring were burgeoning. The main road was virtually empty, and she was able to cross without waiting at all. The situation seemed a bit surreal as if she had woken in some apocalyptic film set in which she was the only person left alive. She walked between two hotels that stood like a pair of grand old ladies looking out over the Channel and she felt a chill as she fell into the shadow of the buildings. She was grateful when she reached The Leas to see that there were dog walkers and joggers and cyclists taking advantage of the fresh air. It looked almost normal but not quite. There were no tourists strolling and no children playing. There were no gardeners tending the flower beds and everywhere was closed up. This felt different from a winter shutdown, more like a retreat. As if the human life of the town had turned in on itself. The seagulls were wheeling and squawking, and the waves were leaping, and it was nature's turn to be in charge now. People were actively stepping aside and moving away from her as she walked. It felt at first as if they were snubbing her but of course they were doing it to everyone. It was a strange thought that every stranger you met could potentially be carrying something deadly if they just breathed near you. Part of her desperately wanted to talk to someone and start making human contact in her new town but it didn't seem an appropriate thing to do in the circumstances, so she just smiled warmly and carried on with her walk. She stood for a while looking out over the sea and watching the sun as it sparkled on the water and had a warm feeling. "This is all mine now,' she thought. "This is my home."

As she walked back to Grimston Gardens she became aware of someone standing looking at her house. As she got closer, she could see that it was a woman. She was wearing a coat buttoned up to the neck on this warm morning. The coat looked old fashioned but possibly vintage. It was lime green boucle material and it was the cut that made it look dated. The woman had shoulder length, dark hair that looked a bit greasy. Her face was pale and slightly pinched looking.

She smiled at the woman as she approached.

"Can I help you?"

The woman started walking up to her and Lisa immediately stepped back to keep a two-metre distance. This startled the woman and she stopped and looked anxious.

"My boy."

"I'm sorry I haven't seen any children out today. I have just moved in here, so I am probably not the best person to ask. How old is he and what does he look like? If I see him where can I find you? Are you a neighbour?"

The woman started wandering away and disappeared around the corner.

As Lisa went to unlock the door of her new flat, she was aware of a lingering smoky smell in the air and was a bit put out to think that the woman had been smoking in her doorway. She put it out of her mind and went indoors. She was going to make a drink and then she had a Zoom meeting with her boss at 11.

Zoom was still quite a new experience for Lisa, and it took a few moments for her to get everything set up. She wasn't officially back at work yet but wanted to touch base with her boss to find out what the plans were for working from home. She hadn't touched her work laptop since before the move and she had to think for a moment to recall the correct password.

The little whirly thing went round and round for a minute or two and then her boss's face appeared on the screen and her own face appeared in a little box in the corner.

"Hi Celia. All this seems a bit strange, but it is good to see you."

"Hi Lisa. How's it all going? Are you all sorted following the move? Do you still think you made the right choice to move to Folkestone?"

"Oh yes, I'm loving it here and the flat is even better in real life and I have so much space."

"Well you certainly look rested. Not as if you have been through the stress of moving house. It must be the sea air!"

The next twenty minutes were focussed on new work practices and how long Lisa could work from home and whether she might have to be furloughed if lockdown was extended.

"That is enough about work stuff for the moment, our time limit will be up in a minute. I can see some of your new flat behind you in the background and it looks very nice, but you are a bit of a dark horse having a cleaner in already. I didn't think we were allowed to have any visitors now we are locked down."

"What do you mean, Celia? I haven't got a cleaner. I am on my own."

"Well I could definitely see someone pottering around behind you on an off while we were talking. She appeared a couple of times. A woman, a bit dowdy looking, could she be one of your new neighbours?"

Lisa whipped her head round to look behind her but there was nothing to see. Everything looked normal.

"There's definitely no one here Celia, just me and I don't have any neighbours in the building at present. The upstairs flat is still unoccupied."

"Oh, I don't know. It looked like someone to me. Maybe it is something to do with Zoom, you do hear of strange things sometimes and meetings being hacked into. Are you sure your security software is up to date? Just get it checked out and I will see you again at the team meeting on Monday. I will send you the link. Bye"

Celia disappeared from the screen and Lisa felt a shiver. She stood up and looked purposefully around the whole flat and everything was absolutely normal. The doors were locked and there was no sign of anyone having been there but herself. Before she shut down her laptop, she upgraded her security software to the highest level.

On Saturday Lisa decided to venture out to a supermarket to get some milk. She found a footpath that gave her a quick walking route to Morrisons. The supermarket was big and looked new. Whilst she was queuing to go in, she asked the woman in front if it was a new store and was told that the whole place had been rebuilt following a huge fire just over a year ago. She made a note to look it up when she got home. She picked up some milk and a nice loaf from the bakery. There was a small display of bedding plants and she picked out a couple of trays of pansies. Strictly speaking they weren't essential purchases, but she wanted to christen her first garden.

When she got home, she treated herself to a couple of slices of warm bread and butter from the new loaf and a mug of tea. She stood at the French windows, the steam from her mug condensing slightly on the glass and noticed again the bare patch in the middle of the grass. That is where I will put my pansies, she thought.

The air smelled sweet and woody and it was just on the cusp of being warm in the sun although it was still chilly in the shade. She knelt down and started digging in the mixture of ashes and earth that made up the bare patch. She planted out her pansies and watered them in. She stood back and admired her handiwork. It looked really good and certainly added some much-needed colour to the garden. She took a picture on her phone and sent it to her mum.

Later in the evening she looked up "Morrisons Folkestone" on Google and watched a news video of the roof collapsing in the fire.

The following morning Lisa opened the curtains, expecting to see the bright flash of colour from the pansies, and had a shock. The pansies looked dead. She pulled on her dressing gown and a pair of trainers and went outside for a closer look. The plants were still alive – just, but they were brown and crinkled at the edges and dry. They looked as if they had been burned. She couldn't understand it. Yesterday they had been bright and colourful and sturdy and now they were dying. What had she done wrong? She bent down and sniffed, and they even smelt as if they had been burned. She went and got her phone and looked at the pictures she had taken yesterday. It was hard to believe it was the same plants. She took some more pictures and decided to ring her mum.

"Hi Lisa. You're an early bird for a Sunday morning. Is something wrong?"

"Mum, you know about gardening, don't you?"

"Well I wouldn't say I'm an expert, but I reckon I know a bit. Why?"

"You know those pansies that I planted yesterday, I sent you a pic."

"Yes, they looked lovely."

"Well look at them now."

She moved the phone to show her mum the dying remains of the flowers.

"Oh dear, Lisa. What have you done to them?"

"I haven't done anything, mum. This is what they were like when I got up this morning. It looks as if they have been burned."

"I don't know why that should happen. Maybe you're just not good at gardening yet!"

"Maybe you're right. I feel a bit silly now ringing you so early for such a trivial thing."

"Never mind darling, it is always lovely to hear from you. Now you stay safe and keep away from this virus. Love you."

"Love you too mum."

That afternoon she dug up the almost dead pansies and put them in the bin. She couldn't bear to look at them anymore.

The team meeting on Monday morning went better than she had expected. She felt like she had the hang of Zoom now and was less distracted by the image of herself in the corner of the screen. It was odd seeing her colleagues at home. Some were in work clothes, but some had obviously decided to go for the loungewear look. In a few cases odd cats, dogs and children appeared in the background but she didn't have to worry about that until Martin commented about her breaking lockdown rules and having someone to stay.

"You're a sly old thing, Lisa. I thought you said you were living completely on your own, but you've got someone staying with you. I wondered at first if it was a secret lover, but she doesn't really look your type."

"What do you mean, Martin? I haven't got anyone here, male or female. You are just winding me up after what Celia said about me having a cleaner."

"Well, there is someone in the background behind you. Who is it?"

Lisa turned away from her screen and looked behind her. There was definitely no one there.

She looked again at her own face on the screen and enlarged it to look in the background and there was no one there either.

"OK Martin, pack it in. There is no one there."

"Well I saw someone," said Maggie

"And me," said Karen.

"Tell you what," said Martin, "This meeting is being recorded. I will send you a copy of the video and try and get some screen shots of when she is in the background and I will email them to you later today."

"How do I know that you won't doctor them just to spook me?"

"Would I do something like that?" Martin said, holding his hands up in all innocence.

Later that day an email with an attachment pinged through from Martin. It contained a video and some stills. Lisa opened the stills first. In them, she saw herself at her laptop screen against the backdrop of her new living room and there in the background was a woman. She felt cold and wanted to look away. She looked behind her again and everything was as normal. She was alone. She enlarged the screenshot to look more closely at the woman. She looked slightly bent over and she had dark, shoulder length hair that looked a bit greasy. She was wearing a plain jumper and a dark skirt, it was difficult to work out the colour and she had an apron tied round her waist. She was a bit familiar to Lisa, but she couldn't think where she had seen her before. She also looked sort of wrong somehow as if she was in the room but not part of it.

Lisa got up and went to the kitchen and poured herself a large glass of wine before she looked at the video. She watched the video of the meeting with the sound turned off and with her box enlarged on the screen. Throughout the 40 minutes the woman wandered in and out in the background. Sometimes she was holding plates and sometime what looked like bundles of washing. There was definitely something odd about the way she moved because she didn't seem to negotiate the furniture and boxes as Lisa would expect. Sometimes it looked as if she was almost walking through them. In the last few minutes of the video Lisa had a shock. The woman had changed into a coat and suddenly she remembered where she had seen her.

"I'm not sure what to do, mum. That video has really spooked me. It looks so much like the woman I saw the other day, but it just can't be. I have looked online to try and find anything out about the house and the area but there is nothing immediately apparent..."

"Ok darling. Let's just calm down and try and think rationally before you get yourself into a state. How do you actually feel? Have you noticed anything in the flat yourself?"

"Well that's the strange thing, mum. Actually, I still feel really happy here and if I don't think about the video and seeing the woman outside, I don't feel scared at all. I honestly thought it was just workmates messing around. It is unsettling but it doesn't make me feel like I want to leave. If anything, it makes me want to find out who she is."

"I worry about you being there on your own but if you are saying you feel ok then I have to believe you. Just a thought, have you tried contacting the estate agent to see if they know anything about the property. Who did you buy it from?"

"It was sold by a property development firm so I don't know if I can get much information from them, but I will try ringing the agents. I know they are all locked down at the moment, but they might have someone working the phone."

"That sounds like a good plan. Also, I'll ask my friend Debby if she can do some digging online for you. She does something with historical records and old newspapers, so she has access to things that aren't available to us mere mortals. Ring me again at any time if you are worried and let me know how you get on."

Lisa rang the estate agent and after a long message telling her that the branch was currently closed due to the coronavirus lockdown, was eventually transferred through to a real person.

"Hi, Lisa this is Jason. Is there a problem? I thought we were all done and dusted with your sale now."

"Oh, hi Jason, no, there isn't a problem as such, well not with the sale anyway. I was just wondering if you knew anything about the history of the property as I have been having a couple of issues. I know that it was sold by a development company, but do you know who owned it before them?"

"Well it is not something that we usually do, and I am working from home at the moment, but I can have a look at the records for you if you like."

"Thanks Jason, that would be really helpful."

After a few moments, he came back.

"It would seem it was purchased by the property company in February 2019 and that it was a probate sale. There are no other records of the house being sold but that only goes back thirty years. My guess is that it was owned by a family for a long time and the bloke eventually died and it was sold."

"Can you give me the name of the person who sold it to the property company? I was hoping to find out about a woman."

"Sorry, no can do. We don't hold that sort of information and even if we did, we would probably be bound by data protection."

"Oh dear, that seems a bit of a dead end then. I was hoping to find out more about the history of the property and the immediate area."

"Sorry I can't be of more help, Lisa. You could try the Land Registry but that will take a long time. Hang on though, my colleague Jenny grew up in that area. She is working from home today so I will ask her to give you a bell to see if she has any local knowledge."

"Thank you so much Jason, you have been really helpful. I will wait for Jenny's call with eager anticipation. Bye."

Lisa sat at her laptop and got stuck into work and several hours seemed to pass almost without her noticing before her mobile rang.

"Hi Lisa, it's Jenny here from the agency, Jason rang me to see if I could give you any background information on Grimston Gardens."

"Oh, hi Jenny, it's so good of you to get back to me so soon."

"I wondered why you wanted to find out more. Is everything all right with your flat?"

"Oh yes the flat is still wonderful, and I love living here. Just a few little things that made me want to know about the history of the place."

Lisa relayed a few edited highlights of the strange Zoom calls.

"I am sure you think I'm some sort of weirdo who sees things, but it is all a bit strange and there must be a logical reason for it all."

"Well it is certainly odd, and I have never heard of anything like that before but to be honest I can't say I am totally surprised. I always thought there was more to that house than met the eye."

"What do you mean by that?"

"I lived round there as a child and I used to walk past that house every day on my way to the Girls' School. It always looked a bit run down and we used to joke that it was haunted and would dare each other to go into the front garden. I am thinking a good forty odd years ago. There used to be two women who lived there, I think they were sisters and I think there was a little boy as well, but we never really saw him properly. They never spoke to anyone and very much kept themselves to themselves. I remember asking my mum about them and she said that one of the sisters was a bit strange and the other one looked after her. I don't know which of them was the boy's mother; I'm not sure if anyone else knew. We used to see one of them outside the front door smoking. She was always smoking, I don't think it was allowed in the house, so she was always outside."

"What happened to them, do you know?"

"Well, all I know is that one day they were all gone. I asked my mum about it and she wouldn't tell me much, just that something bad had happened and the sisters were gone, and the boy had gone into care. After that the house stayed empty and nothing happened to it until the beginning of last year when it went to auction as a probate sale and was bought by a property developer. Our firm handled the sale."

"I presume ownership must have passed on to the boy who went into care then and he sold it."

"Well maybe but the papers referred to a man that had been the previous owner and died so maybe he died before that. Who knows? It would seem the property had been in the same family since it was built around the early 1900s. When we were dealing with the sale, I got the keys and had a look inside. It was amazing, really old and run down of course but full of beautiful period features. It seemed as if it had hardly changed since it was built."

"I know because it is still full of lots of period features."

"Yes, it was an absolute steal for the developer because that is what everyone is looking for these days as you know. I didn't go in again before you bought it but obviously, I saw the pictures and it looks beautifully done."

"Yes, it is, and I am so pleased with it. And thank you so much for all the background information on the house. It's been useful. Just one last question Jenny, you said that you often saw the woman smoking by the front door, can you remember what she looked like?"

"Hmm, let me cast my mind back. I think she had dark hair but mostly I remember her green coat. She was always wearing a green coat."

Everything was quiet and normal for the next week. Lisa didn't have any more Zoom meetings and she had plenty of work to concentrate on during the day. Every evening she went for a walk, sometimes back up to The Leas and sometimes around other roads in the West End looking at the different architecture of the houses. She went to Morrisons again but didn't buy any more pansies.

She had a ping on her phone to say she had an email. It was from her mum. It was quite long and had an attachment, so she decided to open it on her laptop.

The email said that her mum's friend Debby had found a cutting from the Folkestone Herald from 1976 that mentioned her house and that she might find it a bit upsetting.

She opened the attachment.

Woman dies in fire

A woman was found dead in the back garden of a Grimston Gardens property yesterday. According to the fire service it appeared that she had accidentally set fire to her coat whilst smoking but this is yet to be confirmed. The body of another woman in a state of decomposition was found inside the property. The police do not suspect foul play. A child was also found at the property and is in the care of social services.

Lisa looked out of the French windows at the patch of scorched earth in the garden and cried for both the women who had died there and the boy who had been left behind. She wondered whether the fire was deliberate or an accident and if in the end it really mattered. Mental health issues were treated differently in the past. She wasn't sure what she could do for the distressed woman but at least now she knew a little of her story. It had happened in the past and all she was seeing now were echoes and reflections that would eventually disappear.

She had heard that odd things often happened in periods of high anxiety and the world was certainly anxious at the moment.

She knew that she was happy living in Grimston Gardens despite its sad history and the world was a very different place now. Lockdown would soon be over, and things would return to normal.

3

Death Trap

by Deborah J Jones

The school's red brick frontage looked anything but comforting as, with a testy sigh, Florence Benson let herself in and marched straight into her office. The caretaker had long since gone home, as had the day girls. She was thankful for the cup of strong and sugary tea she had swiftly downed with the boarders, after a discreet chat with Matron. Something stronger – although she only occasionally indulged – would have been even more welcome. She scowled at the pennant above her desk bearing the school motto – "Love and serve." Its message seemed rather vacuous. Did she ever do anything else? Especially the serving bit?

Her hand hovered over the telephone. Three girls missing; all three were what she would describe as "spirited." Two of them were promising hockey players. Sport had never been her thing during her own school days, but she greatly admired those who showed prowess in it. As for the other girl, flashes of brilliance at some subjects, hopeless at others and truculent with it. Not a trio she would have put together. Outside her office window, the wind sang in the trees. It was pitch black outside now. She glanced up at the clock. She could not delay this call much longer.

Of course, there was always scope for mischief when it was Speech Day rehearsal. Some years, against her better judgment, she allowed the older girls to make their own way back to school through town from the Leas Cliff Hall. She tapped her fountain pen thoughtfully on the desk. Perhaps they were hiding somewhere.

The lights flickered and then went out. Resolutely, Miss Benson picked her torch up – it was one of those power cuts which seemed to happen so regularly nowadays - and set off through the school. She and Matron had searched it earlier, when the girls failed to turn up at Clewer, the school boarding house, but the woman did tend to prattle on. She shone a light at the ceiling in the Maths corridor, where, she noticed, the rain was coming in. Negotiating her way past the buckets the caretaker had put in place, she opened the door of each classroom. A heap of grubby science overalls abandoned carelessly at the back of one of the classrooms caught her attention momentarily, but there was nobody there. Her mouth set in a grim line, she headed for the stairs.

She entered a small, cluttered room, used by the language assistants for conversation classes. Shining her torch into the interior, she caught her reflection in the old foxed mirror above the fireplace and recoiled slightly. She was getting old. She jumped at a flapping, fluttering noise. Probably a bird trapped in the chimney, she reasoned, resolving to speak to the caretaker tomorrow. She pounced on a deck of cards lying on one of the desks and pocketed them. Making her way back down the narrow stairs, she stumbled over a blue and grey school scarf. Noting with a grimace the owner's name on the neatly-sewn nametape – she would be sure to mention the girl's carelessness at Assembly tomorrow - she pressed on.

That scarf was what the Domestic Science teacher always referred to as a "death trap." Miss Benson had heard the girls mimicking the woman. It was quite funny really, although one shouldn't laugh. One of her governors had recently described the fabric of the school as "one big death trap." The fire escape outside the French room was a prime example – slippery and rickety. There had nearly been a nasty accident only the other week. High spirits, that's all it was; nothing sinister, despite the rumours she had heard. She had read the riot act to all the girls about pushing and jostling. The school needed money spending on it, there was no getting around it. Slightly out of breath after her perambulations, as she rounded the corner from sick bay, Miss Benson stopped dead.

"Who's there?" she called, angling her torch upwards at the galleries. She thought she could make something out on the top floor, a shadow perhaps. There. Directly above the Latin room. Probably nothing, she reasoned. Lowering her torch, she picked with the toe of her smart court shoe at a mark on one of the white tiles and shuddered at the memory; the girl's long dark hair, spread out around her and the blood, as if she were lying in a red puddle.

It had happened only a year into her headship. A terrible accident, according to the Coroner, and the girl's parents had accepted his verdict. They had been so proud of their Coral, for getting into the Grammar School, and had agreed that she shouldn't have climbed up onto the railing. Miss Benson wondered whether today's parents would be quite so forbearing. She thought of the parents of one of the missing girls and shuddered. Only the other week, the same governor had spoken to her again about the galleries and their dangers, suggesting they should be filled in. Well, she wasn't having that. In just a few weeks, the sixth form girls would be gathering round the railings to sing carols. It was a well-loved tradition. She was not about to spoil it for them.

Her thoughts drifted back to poor Coral. There had been murmurings, among a few of the teachers, and some of the girls, that she was rather unkind. Some of the girls had mentioned a teacher, one they had never seen before, a murmur of "Stand back, girls" just before the terrible accident occurred. The accounts were muddled, and Miss Benson had been inclined to treat them as hysterical stuff and nonsense. Coral's parents had left Folkestone afterwards. A member of staff who had attended the same Baptist church as the family had reported that the mother – a nervy, rather colourless woman - had passed away some years ago. However, Miss Benson had been startled, the other evening at a rare but convivial post-staff meeting drink in the Nailbox, to see Coral's father across the room. Those dark, piercing eyes were unmistakable. There had been a few rather uncharitable comments – more tittle-tattle - at the time of the accident to the effect that he could not have been Coral's father, as he was away on war service at the time of her conception. He had said nothing the other night in the pub, simply raised his pint glass in what appeared to be a mocking salute.

The lights came on again with a flicker. Yet they seemed – was her imagination playing tricks again? – dimmer, reminding her of the old town gas lighting she had grown up with. It was probably something to do with the miners' strike. She hoped the new government would finally be able to sort things out. Drawing her cardigan more tightly around herself, she decided there was nothing for it. She would have to call the police now.

A few hours earlier, Gertrude Newson had been taking advantage of some pleasant and unexpected November sunshine –it still gladdened her heart. Today, she had chosen the Zigzag Path for her walk, just around the corner from the spacious and comfortable apartment she still considered to be hers. She felt safe here. Her old geography teacher's instincts kicked in and she peered closely at the cement – pulhamite, to give it its correct name. To the untrained eye, however, it looked like sandstone. If she wasn't mistaken, there was a piece of an old willow pattern plate in there. Instinctively, she reached out to try and touch it. Then she pulled back.

She thought about the army of young men, back from the trenches, who had been mobilised to build it, to give them something to do. Her brother had made it back but only just, and as a gibbering wreck. He had survived for just a few years afterwards. Her fiancé – dear James, she thought fondly – hadn't made it back at all. And then, like so many others, Gertrude had become part of a band of "surplus women," a brutal phrase coined by some journalist or other. It had stuck.

Teaching had become her passion instead and she had found her niche in Folkestone, almost as close as you could get to France. That had been in the back of her mind when she had travelled down for her interview and it was true. Today, the French coast was so close, you could have reached out and touched it. Ahead she could see a fishing boat and a family of seagulls hovering above. Behind her, the Leas Cliff Hall jutted out. It always looked precarious to her. She paused for a moment and looked round. It must be Speech Day soon; of course, there was always a rehearsal. She could hear the young voices raised in song. She winced at the way the music teacher was pounding away on the piano. Her Headmistress – the redoubtable Venetia Apps – would have winced too. This one – and she had seen a few come and go – didn't seem to be bothered. Perhaps she was more charitable or simply not musical. She wondered whether to turn back and see if she could slip in to watch. Nobody would notice her.

Gertrude stepped aside as a mother and her two toddlers – one on each arm - marched past. No acknowledgement, no thanks, but it was ever thus. She moved on, into what she always thought of as the "wild part," a little steeper and more unkempt. Taking a seat on a bench, she sank back, deep in reverie. One of her fondest memories of her teaching days was of Speech Day, in the Town Hall, when Miss Alice Mary Hunt, lady governor, fellow geographer and intrepid traveller, who had extended the hand of friendship, had asked her to operate the lantern for her slide talk. Afterwards back at the flat, Gertrude had traced, in her atlas, the journey Miss Hunt and her niece had taken on the Train de Luxe.

If things had been different, perhaps she could have followed in her footsteps. She had always had a hankering to cross the globe. The most far flung place she had reached, however, was Ypres, on a charabanc trip to see where poor James had eventually been laid to rest. She had felt terribly sick on the boat. Something else she had discussed, rather shyly, with Miss Hunt, all those years ago on one of those afternoons had struck a chord:

"Is character more important than cleverness?"

Did that still apply today, she wondered? There were more gilt letters than ever on the Honours Board and the cupboard in the hall was crammed full of pennants and shields demonstrating the girls' sporting prowess, but was that all that mattered? Only the other week, on one of her visits, she had taken in hand – nobody else was going to, clearly - a class waiting for their French lesson, especially those girls perched on the fire escape. She chuckled. She might have given some of them a bit of a fright. Her thoughts were interrupted by a girl in a grey mackintosh who had planted herself next to her.

"Excuse me, Miss. Do you mind me sitting here?"

Gertrude looked at her sharply. Not everyone could ...oh well, never mind.

"Of course not, dear," she replied. "Though shouldn't you be at rehearsal?"

The girl pulled a face.

"Actually, I decided I'd slip away while the going was good. I'd rather not go to the next lesson. And.." she lowered her voice. "I am thinking of running away. I haven't made my mind up yet."

Gertrude listened while the girl explained how she had recently started boarding at the school, because her parents' work had taken them back over to France. "I didn't like it very much before, but this is a hundred times worse." An all-too familiar tale, a square peg in a round hole, and some appalling bullying. She tried to think where the phrase came from – "This too shall pass" but decided that didn't matter. It was more important to listen to the girl.

"You'll look back on this in a few years and it will all seem quite trivial," she said, after a while. "You've got a great future ahead of you. Don't ruin everything. I only wish I hadn't."

The girl looked at her curiously, but Gertrude wasn't going to elaborate.

"I think," she suggested, "that if you walk back slowly, the long way round, you'll be back just in time for the end of school."

"That's a good idea." The girl smiled mischievously. "I'll walk along the seafront for a while anyway. I'll definitely miss PE though. Oh dear. How sad. Never mind!" Gertrude's face was blank. She wasn't sure what the girl was on about; perhaps it was a catchphrase from television. What an asset that could have been to her teaching. She had been an avid follower of John Logie Baird and his work on "seeing by wireless." She had even answered one of his advertisements in the newspaper, asking for volunteers to help with experiments. Nothing had come of it though – story of her life. The girl stood up. "It's been nice talking to you – sorry, I don't know your name."

"Miss Newson. Gertrude Newson."

"I'm Annette. Named after my grandmother. They even find that funny. Oh well."

Raising her hand in farewell, the girl set off down the path. Gertrude hoped the girl would be all right. The weather was closing in. She was no stranger to bullying herself. She remembered how the girls had teased her relentlessly about everything. Her clothes, her hair, her accent, the fact that she was unmarried...everything.

As if on cue, two more girls – also clad in grey mackintoshes – appeared. They looked rather similar but, Gertrude decided, that was because they had styled their hair in the same way – flick fringes, something she had heard the girls talk about recently on one of her visits to the school. They both shouted at Annette as she made her way towards the beach.

"Skiving off again? We're going to report you," they chorused. "Look at her. Doesn't she walk funny? What a spaz!"

Annette didn't seem to hear them, but enough was enough. The girls' taunting voices reminded Gertrude of the day when, driven to distraction, she had taken the bus to St Margaret's Bay to clear her head. That had been a clear spring day and she remembered wishing she had brought a camera. There had been a chalk fall, but she had continued down the path, despite the warning from the nice lady and gentleman she had met. She had placed her handbag and hat on a bench while she stepped forward to admire the rock formation. She remembered tumbling over and that feeling of indignation, of having been cheated, that she wasn't ready, that she had more to give.

Noticing that Annette had reached the bottom and had turned right, towards the beach and eventually school, she stood up. The girl's tormentors had, meanwhile, moved off the path and were perched precariously on a ledge, with a sheer drop below. Gertrude moved towards them. In seconds, it was all over. They wouldn't have known a thing. Afterwards, through instinct, she dusted herself down fastidiously. It was getting easier all the time. "Practice makes perfect," she murmured. Humming a jaunty air, she made her way through the town towards the school.

Miss Benson closed the heavy front door on the two policemen and shot the bolts firmly across. She could not help wondering whether what was troubling her was inside and not outside. While she had been talking to the policemen in the hall, she thought she had heard a laugh. A short syllable: "Ha." The policemen didn't seem to have heard it though and had kindly checked the building again for her before they left.

Telling herself in no uncertain terms to get a grip, she sat back down at her desk and put her head in her hands. Tragic accident, parents being informed; somehow it seemed horrifically familiar. The police had found Annette on the beach, happily listening to her transistor radio, oblivious to the weather and the dark. She had been sent back to Clewer with a flea in her ear. It was clear that the wretched girl was telling the truth; she had seen nothing. One thing was odd though – the girl had mentioned meeting a teacher, a Miss Newson. The police had yet to identify and interview this person.

With a shaking hand, she reached into the filing cabinet behind her and drew out the old personnel ledger. There wasn't a huge turnover of staff at the school, something she prided herself on, and the book went back through several decades. In neat cursive script, one of her predecessors had written:

"Gertrude Harriet Newson. 1890-1933. Appointed teacher of Geography 1921. Died following a fall on the cliffs at St Margaret's Bay "while the balance of her mind was disturbed."

Photograph by Jo Richards

4

The Ghostly Future

by Karen Marwood

As I sit, reading from my talking Kindle about a pandemic that swept around the world 50 years ago, I stifle a chuckle about the children not being allowed to go to school. I cannot understand why the parents are complaining about them being at home doing their learning. I do all my learning at home, we have a huge screen in the learning room and from 8 am until 5 pm I do my learning from the teacher on the screen. I can see all the children doing the lesson around the outside of the screen. This teacher called Leta teaches us everything we need to know and that is why I am reading about the pandemic. They did lead a very weird life years ago, even having special days about things like book day and Halloween. That looked fun seeing the children all dressed up. The fireworks, these looked cool as they change the sky all different colours. We have the same sort of thing, but we can just shine our laser up to the sky and push the colour button, making a multitude of colours and shapes fill the sky.

If I don't understand something, I ask my Kindle and it tells me the answer. When I get fed up with reading, it reads to me. I can always put on my laser headset and see pictures of whatever I am learning or reading about. At the end of each month we have an exam then, if we pass, we get a point which goes towards our end of year total. If you fail, then you start the month over again with a different teacher.

I am not sure how I am going to remember all the things they did years ago and what year things happened. It all seems so strange the way they all lived. They even had shops and you had to go out to buy things. We buy everything we need to eat from the talking fridge, and it gets delivered on a conveyor type belt that runs along all the paths in front of your house. It ends up in your kitchen by each cupboard and fridge that it goes in. I normally get the job of putting it away as my elder brother is just too lazy to do anything. He left the learning room last year and now works as a fast ride hologram designer. I don't like putting the game eyes on as it's scary and he is horrible to me and frightens me.

Reading about this Halloween they used to have, it seems very strange they cut pumpkins and then lit them and went around houses saying, "trick or treat.' Why would a ghost, which is a white sheet draped over someone, scare people? The witches flew on a broomstick. This is all very strange, and I don't understand it all. They went to collect sweets from people in their houses. We never see our neighbours; even though we live in a small village called Folkestone all the houses are surrounded by a huge wall. We can have sweets once a month, but they do not look the same, I wonder what the sweets used to taste like? I go and get my headset mask so I can taste and smell what these sweets used to be like. I think I prefer ours, they were very sweet with some tasting a bit like fruits. I look at all the photos of the ghosts and listen to the scary noises that go with it. I then come up with a plan, getting very excited the more I think about it.

When my brother takes a drive to his friend's house, where they play instruments together, not sure what he plays as I have never heard him, I go into his room and get his laser head set then take it to my computer and I program into it lots of ghostly noises and pictures of ghosts appearing in and out of his room. I also go into our house control centre and make his blinds open when the ghost appears, I can put it all on a timer. His doors open and shutting, I am having so much fun and am very pleased with myself for paying attention when we were given a tour of the house and its controls when we came to live here years ago. They also update the system so I can always go to that meeting or listen to it on the big screen. I also plan for the television to screen the scariest movie I can find the following evening as I know we will be home together alone. I also plan in the door bell ringing, microwave starting up and a piercing scream from myself.

My brother is a nasty person at times, always saying cruel things to me and even hitting me sometimes but he never gets caught, he knows all the small places that the house cameras do not reach. He deserves this and it will make him pay for everything he has done to me. I think I would have liked Halloween!

The next night as we are both watching the film, I even make him some popcorn, just to be nice. The film is scary, so I make him jump a couple of times which I find highly amusing. When the film finishes, we both go up to our rooms and I say good night to him. I know he will be playing online games using his laser headset, the ghosts will start appearing then the noises will start. His face appears on my screen and he asks me if I have been playing around with his stuff? Of course, I deny any knowledge by asking him what is going on. That's the precise moment the piercing scream sounds all around the house and he looks at me, realising that it isn't me. As he walks towards his door it opens. I hear him scream like a baby and go running downstairs looking to see if mum and dad are back yet. I sit on the stairs watching him. As he goes in the kitchen the back door opens and the microwave starts up. My brother is standing there crying and has wet himself!

I sneaked very quietly back to my room, stifling my laughter, he so deserved all that. The next day at breakfast he told our parents all about his evening. They laughed as though he was making it up. He then started to tell them about the two people who walked into the kitchen when the back door opened.

"No," I said. "You're dreaming now, there was no one here." He described what they looked like, heads swivelling, eyes bulging, blood running from their mouths. They then walked towards him and he quickly took a photograph on his phone before he ran. He told me it was all true and showed me a photo of two skinny looking ghostly white shapes!

"Who are they?" I said.

"How the hell do I know? But they were here last night," he replied.

5

Return from thc Front

By Carol Harte and Lynzy Heartfield-Brown

On 16th May 1915, Frederick had been travelling for several days in Old Bill, his bus. It had been converted for the war effort and as a British soldier he was very proud to be driving it. He had crossed the English Channel by ferry and was transporting soldiers to the front line to fight in the Belgian province of West Flanders not far from the French border of Ypres. The soldiers he had brought over on his bus were fresh out of training school and were in good spirits and raring to go. They were all singing "Pack up your Troubles in Your Old Kit Bag" and sang out to the tune of the Colonel Bogey March. Many of them had just left the army training camp in Shorncliffe Barracks, Folkestone.

Frederick, who was at the steering wheel in front, joined in with them. The London boys that were recruited for the war effort were as young as fifteen, they had lied about their age to fight in the war. It was heard that a soldier who was just twelve years old was conscripted into the war effort and fought at the Somme at the age of thirteen. Some of the soldiers on Frederick's bus were sick before they saw any fighting action. The hard wheels of Old Bill rattled along on the old cobblestone roads and gave all the soldiers a proper shaky ride. Some buses were converted to ambulances and ammunition vehicles and transported supplies to the front line. Other vehicles had carrier pigeon lofts which stood out in front of the buses above the drivers' seats. They were fully equipped for war.

The second battle of Flanders was taking place in Ypres which included two corps of the British Army, namely 1st Canadian Division, commanded by General Sir Horace Smith-Dorrien. The French 45th (Algerian) and 87th Territorial Division, under General Henri Putz, and the Belgian 6th Division, under Major General Armand de Ceuninck. The rest of the Belgian army headed north to the flooded area where the First Battle of Ypres had taken place. This ongoing battle ran from April-May 1915. A million soldiers from more than fifty different countries were either wounded, missing in action or killed in the whole of World War 1, and as many civilians as soldiers also died at this time. Cities and villages were destroyed by enemy fire and their inhabitants fled to many parts of Europe. Sixty-five thousand Belgian refugees entered Folkestone harbour, homeless and penniless.

When Frederick arrived at the battle zone with all his passengers, he and they saw a bleak landscape, that had experienced heavy shelling and bombardment. Areas covered in barbed wire, dead, broken bodies of soldiers and horses, half submerged in thick mud, and in various stages of decomposition. When the smell hit your nostrils, it was unbearable. The soldiers experienced walking in thick mud sometimes almost up to their knees for nine months of the year.

Frederick looked out of the bus window amidst the singing of the hyped-up soldiers, adrenaline full on. He saw convoys of motor ambulances. Four streams of traffic heading in the same direction along a narrow muddy road towards Ypres. Comprising of ammunition and supply vehicles carrying bandages and other medical supplies, blankets and tins of bully beef. Emergency postmen and messengers on wobbly bicycles were economical to run, they didn't need feeding like horses. Then came British, Belgian and Canadian soldiers marching behind one another, looking weary and exhausted. Along came the runners darting in and out amongst the horses pulling the ambulances, trying not to scare the animals.

Getting themselves half stuck in mud more than anything else. Some Scottish soldiers from the Gordon Highlanders dressed in dark kilts sang out to snatches of Harry Lauder, sounding beautiful but eerie. Frederick's eyes scanned the whole scene, he was mesmerised by the atmosphere. Soldiers, going into battle. A heavy built ammunitions lorry struggling along with heavy metal guns that stuck out like telescopes, looking formidable and dangerous, waited patiently as soldiers passed by before attempting to manoeuvre this huge monstrosity onto the main road. Enemy shell firing had just started along with a heavy downpour of rain.

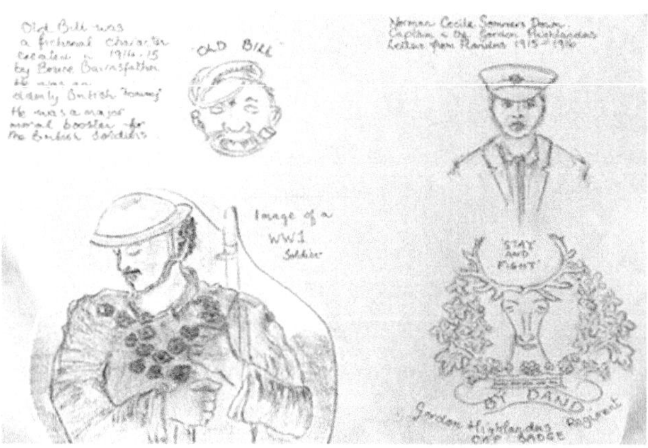

Some English-speaking soldiers stopped and spoke to Frederick as his head protruded out of the bus window.

One of them said: "Back up the road they've got soldiers on sentry guard protecting the town of Ypres." It was heavily bombarded, villagers left, shop windows smashed to bits. "They got to protect the place against looters!" Nearby, a group of Scottish pipers started up into a rendition of "Highland Laddie" and a huge cheer went up from all the soldiers comprising of businessmen, road sweepers, stevedores, students and office clerks. All fighting for their country. Frederick and his soldiers on the bus cheered along too. The atmosphere was electric.

The convoy of traffic consisting of soldiers, horses and vehicles tried to increase their speed on hearing the shelling. Frederick fell in line, with Old Bill. There was a clearing to the left between large trees and bushes and he could see a group of soldiers who were shouting in their direction and waving their arms about. They had obviously seen battle, some had heavy bandages around limbs and heads, and some had been blinded by the chlorine gas that the Germans had introduced, and they had shrapnel wounds. Another soldier was shaking fiercely. The soldiers were more noticeable by their injuries rather than their rank of division.

A junior officer near the injured soldiers beckoned Frederick to drive his bus towards them. He was only young, exhausted and jaded.

"Get those virgin soldiers off that bus and take these lads home. They've done their bit for their country!" Frederick saluted. The fresh soldiers quickly scurried off the bus with their basic equipment, with pink cheeks reminiscent of chubby babies' bottoms, to allow the injured soldiers to get on. They all shook hands with each other and the badly injured were patted on the back. The new guys were immediately given loaded rifles and sent into action. Frederick and the junior officer quickly helped the injured soldiers onto Old Bill. The rain and the shelling began to subside. The less injured were encouraged upstairs to the open top of the bus, they had to cover their heads from the rain and enemy fire. The junior officer jumped off the bus and shouted to Frederick:

"Turn the bus around and head straight back to Calais!!" The officer threw two crates of Belgian beer into the back of the bus, the bottles had short necks and red labels. All the soldiers cheered.

"We're going home lads! "shouted Frederick from the front of the bus. There were more appreciative noises from the men. The soldiers appeared to be British, French and Belgian and there were two Indian Sikhs who sat at the back of the bus. They wore their impressive turbans and fought under the British Raj. Before long Frederick was back along the familiar road he had driven in on. Gradually pulling away from the battle zone. It was getting dark and a thick fog came down restricting his view ahead. His lights weren't doing a good job in dealing with the weather. The more able soldiers handed around the bottles of beer. Frederick passed back a bottle opener from the top pocket of his uniform. The soldiers shouted for joy.

"Well done soldier," the two Sikhs waved from the back. Some of the soldiers started to strike up a conversation, they began to relax. They were going home.

Frederick could hear the conversations from the front of the bus; as he drove along past dead soldiers and several abandoned ambulances, the soldiers were retelling their experiences of fighting on the front line.

"We'd been marching for a long time," a Canadian soldier spoke up. "Tired and exhausted, we just wanted to rest, we then had to dig trenches, but at least we were safe. We were shelled continuously for hours." Usually the trenches were bombed during the day and rebuilt during the night, allowing little time for sleep. He continued: "Then we heard our battalion was returning home to reform and recruit. The good news came to us after nineteen days on the battlefield and didn't actually happen until we had been out there for twenty-six days."

Jock spoke up, a Gordon Highlander in a kilt, and a heavily bandaged leg. He had walked onto the bus with a bad limp and he had dried mud all over his uniform and his face: "I'd been suffering badly from lack of sleep before I was injured. My mate made me a mug of hot cocoa in a billycan, as I held the hot mug in my hand, I dropped off to sleep spilling the hot liquid down my bare legs. That's why my leg is bandaged from the hot burning liquid, inflicted by myself."

Near the back of the bus was a soldier sitting quietly but for the constant tapping on the window with his rifle that he had firmly clenched in his hands. A soldier spoke up: "He can't help it, a shell went off close to him, didn't kill him but covered him in earth. He's not stopped shaking since, he's my neighbour back in London, I gotta take care of 'im."

Frederick called back. "I'm stopping the bus guys; I've got to look in the engine. It seems to be overheating." The Scotsman shouted: "It's all that mud slowing us down!!" The Sikhs laughed. Frederick got out and went to the front of the bus and lifted the side hood, smoke was billowing out. He yelled out. The handbrake wasn't on and he slowly slipped under the front of the bus as it rode over him.

A soldier shouted: "The bus is moving forward. Where's the driver?" Another soldier, sitting near the front, managed to grab the handbrake and with all his limited strength pulled it upwards.

Frederick was dead in the mud. Two soldiers managed to pull him onto the bus, and they found an old blanket and covered him over. The soldier with the shakes began to cry loudly. Jock shouted out: "Of all the ways to die in this stinking war, he dies under his own bus." There was silence for five minutes as they thought of Frederick who had just lost his life until Jock shouted again:

"Can anyone drive this bus?"[1]

On Saturday 17th May 1941, thunder rumbled in the distance and fork lightning penetrated the murky sea mist. Life had changed dramatically in the Folkestone area, and many families with young children had been evacuated to Wales, but some elderly residents remained in the town even though they were in a vulnerable location, very close to the French coast, where the Germans were launching their attacks on the English South Coast. They were content to stay in their homes and a visit to the theatre was a tremendous distraction from the constant bombing raids.

The weather conditions deterred many enthusiastic locals from attending the 1927 built Leas Cliff Hall that evening and theatre goers were thin on the ground. It was previously called The Leas Shelter, which was much smaller, seating only two hundred people but The Grand Hall in the Leas Cliff Theatre had ample seating for nine hundred with almost double the amount of standing room.

Those who arrived for the performance were dressed in their finery, which for many was their Sunday best, if they had been fortunate enough to still have it, as they were on their way to watch the greatest tenor of the twentieth century. He wore a monocle which disguised a squint, but which complemented his debonair appearance, and he used his breath control to produce the most delightful musical experiences known to audiences throughout the world. Austrian born, Richard Tauber, was the most prolific opera performer of his time and had sold many gramophone records and most of the audience arriving for the afternoon matinee adored him. One of his most famous songs was "You are my Heart's Delight," from the operetta Land of Smiles.

They queued for a short time outside the modern theatre, where soldiers had previously been lined up in readiness to march to Christchurch in Sandgate where a parade was taking place in honour of two women parishioners killed by the previous week's shelling. Colourful posters were displayed on the ornate red flock covered walls, one advertising forthcoming theatre performances and another encouraging people to join up to fight in the war. The ticket prices were also listed on the wall beside the kiosk and cash was used to pay for seats. A plaque on the wall celebrated the opening of the theatre by Prince Henry, Duke of Gloucester. The audience took their seats, settling down and breathing in the luxury surrounding them: the gold leaf embossed ceiling; the magnificent plush red velvet drapes hanging from the balconies surrounding the private boxes and the heavy curtains drawn across the almost fifty-foot stage.

Richard Tauber was waiting in the wings and he would certainly have been disturbed by the dwindling in audience numbers for the evening, due to the bad weather conditions and the recent shelling along the south coast, when the stage door slammed open and lightning ripped through making contact with some copper plumbing pipes situated behind a cabinet containing

---

[1] In the summer of 1915, a free buffet called "The Mole Café" was set up on Folkestone Harbour Arm, offering free refreshments to soldiers, sailors and red cross workers and it was run by local volunteers.

In December 1915, the spy Margaretta Geertruida Zelle, known as Mata Hari was stopped from boarding a ship at Folkestone Harbour by Captain S Dillon, of the Secret Service.

In 1918, the Mayor of Folkestone reported 8.6 million passengers during 1914-1918: troops en route to France, returning from leave and travelling red cross workers. Folkestone Harbour was also the preferred route for war mail, transporting documents of importance and letters to and from soldiers at the front. There were 10,500 ships and 7,000 train movements for military use.

musical instruments, the doors of which flew open, causing a massive clatter as trumpets, trombones, bugles and euphoniums fell to the floor.

Molly was already seated in the front row of the stalls beside a married couple around her age which led her to ponder over William and how different life would have been had he lived. Her thoughts were interrupted by the tremendous noise coming from behind the stage and she was surprised when she suddenly noticed a young soldier sitting beside her. He was very polite, saying good afternoon to her as he removed his cap. She thought how handsome he was, just like William at his age. The only difference being that the young soldier had striking blue eyes, whereas William's were brown, but his stature was similar. They were both of medium height with mousey coloured hair.

She wondered what could have caused the noise and the soldier said it sounded as if Richard Tauber had brought in the Keystone Cops to accompany him. Molly thought the comment hilarious and laughed out loud while glancing at the soldier who had delivered the comment with a deadpan expression on his face and by this time had produced a bag of toffees from his pocket. He gave her a disgruntled look, raised his eyebrows and shook his head as he offered her a toffee.

"Thank you, I shouldn't really, they get stuck in my false teeth," she laughed, taking one whilst introducing herself:

"I'm Molly, mother of six".

"Six," he exclaimed. "I have two young'uns myself. My name is Frederick. You're a Londoner too, aren't you"?

"Yes, from the Old Kent Road originally. I was brought up there, met my husband William, a train driver, who moved in with my family, until we could find somewhere suitable to live. I lost two children, so as you can imagine, times were hard. William unfortunately died with the cancer in 1920. He was only 41. We had recently moved to the Leas because his train came into Folkestone Junction and he found the house during one of his breaks before the train boarded the boat to France. I managed to cope because I had a hard upbringing, left school at fifteen, had to help mother about the house and help her to look after my younger brothers and sisters. She took in washing and minded children, so I gained plenty of experience in that department".

Frederick laughed as he continued chewing his toffee.

"I don't live far from there. I drive my bus along the Old Kent Road. Life's been good to me really, 'til now that is, a beautiful wife and a son and daughter and just bought a three-storey house near Clapham Junction, Battersea, and we want more children when this blessed war ends."

"You've done very well for a young man. I don't suppose you get home to see them very often, "Molly said.

"No, I've been driving "Old Bill" a lot, taking the troops over."

Molly didn't understand but nodded. *Who is old Bill*, she thought? "Taking the troops over where"?

She thought he mumbled "*Flanders*."

"Are you looking forward to seeing Tauber? I've listened to his singing. It's always on in the canteen - songs from Carmen and Tosca."

"Yes, I adore him, I find listening to him so relaxing. My children clubbed together to buy my ticket today. They've done it before. Of course, they're all grown up now. My eldest is a schoolteacher," she added proudly, reminiscing at how her dream had been to do just that. She was immensely proud of them. "My other daughter lives in Queen Street and was almost shaken out of her bed when a shell landed in Clarence Street last year. Tommy, my grandson, later found a piece of shrapnel, the nose cap of the shell, which he's kept as a souvenir." Molly's voice trailed off, as the curtains opened to loud applause and Richard Tauber appeared on stage.

They both appeared to be enjoying the performance, constantly exchanging nods and smiles.

Frederick told Molly how the last time he was at a theatre was to see a review of "Everybody's Doing It" with music by Irving Berlin and Cuthbert Clarke, at the Empire Theatre, Leicester Square, two years before the war and she gleaned from that that he was a keen theatre goer,

Molly excused herself to visit the lavatory during the interval. She noticed the couple sitting next to her looking at her strangely when she returned to her seat and she felt behind her to make sure that her dress wasn't tucked into her pink bloomers. Something she did when returning from the outside toilet at home, causing much laughter amongst her children. Frederick wasn't in his seat, but she caught a glimpse of him slowly walking up the aisle towards her, carrying what looked like two ice creams in cardboard tubs which she assumed he had just purchased from the usherette standing in front of the stage holding a tray, secured by a strap that hung around her neck. She wondered how he could have bought them as rationing was in place and it was difficult to get an allowance for sweets, unless you had rationing coupons, and confectionery was mainly made available for children, as many of the older generation handed in their coupons "for the little ones." He slowly sat down beside Molly and her eyes glistened as they glazed over with tears of happiness when he handed an ice cream tub to her, evoking memories of William when they had sat in a theatre many years before.

When the performance had ended, she turned to say goodnight to Frederick and to wish him well on his travels to the front, but he had gone. She asked at the kiosk on the way out of the theatre, but the assistant told her there were only a few people in that afternoon and that she would have remembered if there had been a soldier and that she hadn't seen any in that afternoon.

Illustrations by Lynzy Heartfield-Brown

6

East Cliff

by Andrew Paul

Rita sat down in her overripe armchair. She wiggled her shoulders and settled back and set the tray on her lap. A tv dinner was a rare treat; she tended to eat sparingly and on the run. She did not as a rule count herself as a food person. She glanced up at the heavy-set mantelpiece and her eyes got a little dusty at the old black and white photograph of her lost collie Casey. She turned the television on and sought distraction. Her left hand rested against the arm and she could feel the wear in the fabric where Casey had rubbed his back when sat beside the chair. It was the reason she had never replaced the armchair.

Casey had been a rescue pup, a busy ball of nose, whiskers and paws that had were a little too big for his frame and he had chosen Rita and she had been happy to have been chosen. He had arrived at the right time; Rita's elderly mother had died, and Rita was alone in the tall narrow terrace, a brisk five-minute walk from the East Cliff.

As the years rolled on, Rita's life had revolved around work, walks and Casey and their favourite walk had been along the East Cliff, around the old white faced and crumbling Martello Tower and down towards the long sweep of the coast to the harbour, where, every Friday, Rita had brought a fresh plaice or dab for her evening meal and a bag of bones for Casey.

In the late autumn of Casey's seventh year with Rita, the usual routine came to an end when, off the lead, Casey set with a will to chasing a rabbit who had ventured up onto the cliff top. Ears flat and tail bobbing; the rabbit had rounded the Martello Tower at a rate of knots and slipped into the creeping rise of the undergrowth. Casey followed racing hard, his breath pumping, his paws trying to gain purchase on the freckled frost of the sloping grass; he missed the turn and in a scrabble of paws, flailing tail and a painful yelp had fallen away over the edge and into the heavy dark bellied sea. Rita had stood on the edge, the tops of her shoes slipping a little in the crumbling of chalk and grass, but she had not seen Casey again. His last cry lived on in her memory and in her dreams.

Rita had never been quite the same. She had quietly stepped back from the world. Friends had suggested she find a new dog, but she could not bring herself to do so; in some obscure way it never seemed quite right. She continued to walk but she avoided the route she and Casey had followed, she had followed the old tram road down into town instead, it was easier that way. She had more than once thought she had seen a collie trotting on ahead of her or felt the press of a warm flank into her hip; but there had never been a dog there when she looked again.

Rita had mentioned those "sightings" as she called them to her brother on his weekly visit. He had laughed and dismissed them, and Rita had not mentioned them again. She kept them close to herself in some faint echo of hope or warmth in her diminishing world.

Rita had retired early; without regret or thought. She had begun to dislike the atmosphere in the office; the sense of unease amongst the younger members of staff who saw little prospect of long-term employment. She told herself she was making way for someone but in truth she was seeking retreat. She liked to lock her front door and potter around the house without seeing a soul, snacking now and then on tea and toast and wondering how much clearer the past seemed to her than tomorrow ever could.

Rita's brother had found her in her armchair on his final visit. She had simply stopped. He gave her a hug of farewell but there was nothing of her in her body any longer. She had slipped away, as private and discreet as ever, with the old picture of Casey on her lap.

The funeral at Barham had been sparsely attended and Rita's brother had placed the photograph of Casey in his sister's coffin. He had read the eulogy and as his last words faded away into the shadows and beams, he could have sworn he heard the click of a dog's nails on the stone of the chapel floor and more distantly his sister's gentle chuckle which has always reminded him of water in a slow chalk stream. He laughed at himself and laughed a little less certainly when, on leaving to collect his car, he thought he had spotted a collie through the trees. He had sat behind the wheel of his car for a long moment before turning the key in the ignition and switching on the car stereo; he pressed play and the first note of "A Lark Ascending" somehow seemed appropriate for the mood and the moment. He had nosed the car out of the car park and then out through Denton and all too quickly back to Folkestone. He stopped at the Lifeboat Inn on returning to Folkestone for something medicinal and then a second and a third. He had been required to take a taxi home.

Rita's brother returned rarely to Folkestone after his sister's death other than to complete the clearance of her house; he found little of value or worth, but several hoards of pound coins and a photograph of Rita and Casey taken by a neighbour. He kept the photograph and gave the coins to charity.

His final task was to scatter Rita's ashes and he had, after a period of reflection, decided to return her to the East Cliff, so late one evening in early winter he stood by the Martello Tower in the half light and released her ashes to the high winds. He murmured a farewell and then strode across the grass to his car and drove away without looking back.

Rita's brother did not see Rita and Casey walking along the East Cliff. His sister was smiling, and Casey was close in at her flank where he belonged. He had waited and she had found him, and they walk together in the half-light...

7

Broomstick

by Karen Marwood

The broomstick lies, alone and unloved

The tears form, sliding down

How do you get so battered and bruised?

I ask as I sit all alone.

Feeling detached

Wiry hair all stiff

Some falling out

Not needed at all

The body is scratched

From years of abuse

The hands that held it

Not caring at all.

8

Five Times the Devil came to Folkestone

by Aleksandra Michalska

In Martello tower no. 3 –

I'm speaking of the one on the golf course, the one that's decrepit and graffiti covered, the one managed by the Creative Foundation –

In Martello tower no. 3, there is a portal to Hell. It is the last building in town, overlooking the ocean on one side and Folkestone on the other, and as such it is the portal to Hell. It is customary it would be – the last house, the last staircase, the last door and window in town. This is where the Devil comes through.

He wants you to wonder why Folkestone, and so let us wonder. Firstly, we could say He likes the water. The coming and going of tides. A peaceful interlude from the constant screaming of His home. More so even from all the paperwork – souls come with a lot of it, demons come with even more, and the man upstairs likes to keep strict deadlines. Maybe He'd been prescribed a dose of iodine by some-or-other hell-bound doctor.

Or maybe it's the fields, stretching up Canterbury-way, Ashford-way. The greenery, the ancient woods, the rolling hills of Kent so often spoken of in songs.

You'd ask: why not London? London would make more sense. More people, more, well, everything. Why not go to London and turn the North Circular into more of a flaming hell than it already is?

And the answer: why *not* Folkestone?

And so, He comes to Folkestone, in 1802 or thereabout once the Tower is finished. The builders notice a shadow appear, a smell in the air like of curiosity (a dark kind, the type that kills the cat) the moment they lay down the last brick. They think nothing of it. Strange smells are not unusual in Folkestone. The shadow is a different matter, when it grows and becomes less a shadow and more a shape, and then there is a man standing where no man was before. There is a hint of hooves and of horns, and an aura of red, but then there isn't. He looks like an accountant.

"It ain't ready yet," one of the men says, then mumbles angrily about pushing deadlines and cuts and how at this rate, with what they'd been given in way of resources and budgets, the Tower will collapse when someone sneezes come five years. The Devil smiles because He knows that it won't.

The other men agree. There are five of them, each covered in various building substances and smelling mildly of lead. It's in the paint. The sky breaks into a storm and the Devil sighs, comfortably, together with thunder crashing through the field (it's a field now, the golf course won't come till much later). It happens sometimes, if it's been a while since He'd come up. It feels a bit like releasing pressure from joints, stiff knuckles: a little bit of pain, a whole lot of relief.

"Oh, bugger it to hell," the same man says. The Devil knows his name is John. "Can't paint in this. Pack up, lads, I'm calling it a day."

The others follow, since John is the foreman. They seem pleased enough to get the day off. The youngest one stops halfway through putting his brushes away, looks up at the Devil, says: "Are you staying in town, mister? Can't be out here in this weather." He offers to show the Devil the way to an inn.

The Devil accepts. They walk through the field, first stopping off at the young man's house. It's just one room, and inside his wife and a baby, and a non-descript elderly relative. The baby cries in the wife's arms, while she cooks, and the elderly relative watches the rain pouring down the window. The young man is soaked to the bone, and so is the Devil, and it's an unpleasant feeling, sticky and hot, but cold, and claustrophobic. He remembers why He doesn't come to England much.

The wife says they can't go back out in the downpour. The young man, whose name is Jack, says with the weather the inn will run out of rooms. The wife convinces them to stay for tea. The Devil doesn't speak, He observes and listens, and wills the baby to stop crying. It does.

"Annabella must like you," says the wife, handing Him the baby as if He were not a stranger, but a friend. The Devil is surprised. It's not often that the humans hand him something, usually trying to barter or rage or beat him at games of chess, just to *not* give him *anything*. He doesn't particularly like chess, either. The air colours with His confusion.

The baby is wriggly and heavy, as if all the weight of a person was condensed into a too-small body, like a neutron star. He worries He will drop it, but it's an unfounded worry that comes from nowhere – He had never dropped anything before, in the millions and billions of years of existing. It wouldn't do, being a clumsy Devil.

Annabella, who Jack calls Bella, affectionately, watches His face as if she alone understood just who He is, and all the universe, too. There is a galaxy inside her eyes.

The Devil wonders about the name. It's French, which is ironic considering what her dad is building. The Tower also carries a French name, but misspelt. Mortella, Martello. The English can be fascinating in their arrogant blindness, the Devil thinks. (He likes to generalise as much as the next man.)

The wife makes tea as Jack changes into dry clothes as Annabella holds His thumb tightly, urgently, as if to convey a message.

Nobody dies in England for a week, after this, but this is before the internet, or wide-spread newspapers, so no one notices.

*

It's many years before the Devil comes through the Martello Tower no. 3 portal again. It's starting to ruin but holds intact longer than John the Foreman predicted. He hadn't lived to see it past the five-year mark, this the Devil knows for a fact. The Tower had never once been used in combat.

It's now 1849. The train station on the Folkestone Harbour has just opened for the public. The Devil walks towards it, through the mud which clings to His boots. He's wearing modern clothes, more comfortable than the breeches from His last visit, and marvels at the top hat. It frames His features well, if He says so Himself.

A train pulls into the station. It's a passenger train. Ladies in dresses are waving white cloth napkins at the young lads settling themselves into the carriages. The Devil hopes no French are around to see this act of surrender, then remembers He's in the rare time period when no such worries are necessary. No war going on right now, not here anyway. There will be one soon, again, and then again, He knows, but for now the ladies are free to wave their white flags around with no fear of being misinterpreted.

A girl sells tea and cakes from a shabby table. It's too strong for His liking and leaves a black residue on the cups, which she has nowhere to wash after use, so instead they get precariously stacked in columns of five, six, seven even, after the ladies in dresses and men in suits return them. The Devil pulls out a few coins from His pocket and hands them to her. There are always coins in His pocket, and always the exact amount He needs. It's a handy trick.

The girl pours him tea from a pot covered in a grey knitted cosy and asks if He'd like sugar with it. She hands it to Him, a heavy stoneware mug filled to the brim. The Devil notices her eyes have galaxies in them and wonders how long it's been. Too long, but He knows better than most that if you wait long enough you can see the same features in different people. The guy upstairs has limited imagination and likes to use tricks such as genetics to make up for it. That's why all fish look fish-like, and everything around is more or less the same shape – head, spine, arms, legs.

Now that He'd noticed it, there is a lot about the girl that reminds Him of Jack, and of his wife, and even of the useless elderly relative, but all of them must be long dead. The baby too, maybe, He isn't certain.

"Are you from around here?" the girl asks, and now He knows her name is Martha. She asks because He doesn't look it, and because people who are rarely buy her tea. Why would they, when their own is just a few minutes away?

He tells her no, and she doesn't pry. Martha is a pretty girl, although harassed-looking, and He wonders what Annabella looked like when she was grown. He could check, of course, but something about it doesn't sit right in his chest. Remembering her as a baby with a strong, telling grip would suffice.

Martha asks if the tea is fine, because He hadn't drunk any of it yet and so He drinks. It's strong enough to strip the enamel of His teeth, but of course His teeth don't work quite like that. He tells her it's fine, and she makes small talk about the weather while pouring a cup for someone behind Him. The Devil steps sideways to allow the annoyed man through. He'd not noticed He was in the way, and it's a weird feeling of hidden, burning shame that has no place to exist. If the red-faced man wanted Him to move, he could have asked, but the Devil feels that somehow, He missed some form of a cue He should have followed in this intricate British queuing business. His own tea, and the one Martha poured for the man, and her teapot, all get saturated through with the repressed indignation He is feeling. Nobody will enjoy it now.

A few weeks later some lesser-known headlines claim all tea in England had been contaminated, because some people say: "it just doesn't taste right". This gets dismissed at large, because although the claim is correct, nobody wants to be the one to say so.

**

In the 1900s, at the beginning of the century, the Devil comes again. He's not too sure what year it is exactly, only that the huge monstrous building of a new hotel named aptly The Grand has just been finished.

He's standing at the cliff edge, looking up at the structure, blinded by sunlight and it's so loud all around from what seems to be hundreds of tourists He considers turning back and never coming again. There is now a family living at Tower no. 3, and He gave the mother a brief fright when He appeared. That in itself is not an issue – He ensured her of His only intention (checking if the storm-battered window isn't damaged) and she believed immediately, but then He had to actually *do it,* check out the window, and then the brickwork because she was concerned about something, and then something else. It was a hassle, and a town which is no longer quiet might not be worth that hassle.

He walks to the building up the stairs through the door into the dining room, and from afar He knows already what He's about to see, because the girl at the window is looking right at Him with eyes that hold galaxies, although she is blind. He tries not to know her name but it's too late, she is singing, and He knows. Luna, for the moon, and Martha is dead, and so is Martha's daughter, and Luna is only young, but she looks at Him as if she knows.

He's being ridiculous and sentimental, but Her voice is lovely and before He knows it He's at a table in a corner, with a cup of tea and a slice of cake, and the tea is nothing like Martha's, and nothing like Annabelle's mother's, and he knows that twice is coincidence, but three times is the work of the Devil, but since He is the Devil then He doesn't know whose work this is.

He does not speak to Luna, but He feels she sings to Him. Although there are others in the café she does not once take her unseeing eyes off Him. She sings of things He shouldn't understand, like love and the sea and longing, and all of a sudden He understands them, and they seep out of Him with such a strong wave a lady at the nearest table starts weeping into her handkerchief, telling her husband *I don't know why, nothing is wrong, it's just this song... I'll go lie down.*

(This is lucky for her, because it reminds her of feelings she'd long forgotten, and it brings colour back into her life, and that of her husband's, and they go travelling together until they die, younger than they would have had they stayed, but happy.)

Luna sings another song, then another, and the Devil drinks tea after tea from intricate porcelain cups, poured by delicate hands. Luna is bathed in golds and pinks of the sunset, and the Devil understands now why there is so much glass at the front of the building. The light sets her pale hair on fire.

Around Him, patrons switch from tea to gin and whiskey, and He nods the waiter for one, too. Right now, as is the fashion, the Devil has a thick moustache curled up at the ends, and a bead of whiskey forms on it. Luna sings a happier song, laughs at the chorus and the Devil is certain she is laughing at Him.

Instead of bringing the building, or town, or county to sea level, the Devil laughs too, although quietly enough that no one else can hear Him.

Some years later, the man who built The Grand becomes the Mayor, fulfilling his life-long dream.

***

The Devil waits a hundred years before He returns. He thinks about it long and hard. A hundred years is four generations, and four generations is enough for whatever design has been made to pass. He looks for signs it passed: no more women with galaxies in their eyes born and no more of them dying. But the sign doesn't come, He loses His patience, curiosity wins, He appears in Tower no. 3 again. Nobody lives there anymore, and there are spiders in corners the size of His fist, and the smell of mildew. He has to break the door to get out. The Harbour train station had been closed, and re-opened, then closed again.

The Devil made sure to miss all major happenings, but forgot that a new millennium was starting, or had started, and that there was an end-of-the-world prophecy nobody could agree on the date for. 2000, for some, 2001 for the rest. He comes in December 2000, on New Year's Eve, to watch the fireworks.

Folkestone is not what He remembers. Marine Crescent has windows boarded up with breezeblocks. The Harbour Arm, where Martha once sold her tea, is derelict and closed to the general public. He walks down the Leas, looks into the great glass front of The Grand where Luna sang – there is a piano there now, but the pianist plays badly and the same few songs in a loop. Nobody stays from teatime into alcohol-time.

The Devil rummages in His jeans pocket, and surely finds what He is looking for: a brick shaped mobile phone with a black-and-green screen, which somehow manages to connect to the internet. There is an article on the BBC which takes fifteen minutes to load, all about the Channel Tunnel and how it "sucked all life" from Folkestone. The Devil feels something He never felt before Luna had sung, but now it's diluted and tinged with regret. "I found Folkestone so depressing I had to move to Canada," says a comment on the article. The Devil is angry at the sentiment, but then again how can He be, when He had not been there for a hundred years. Had He not run away, too?

There is a tent at the Leas, far from where the public would go, where fireworks are being prepped. The Devil walks into it, having found nowhere else to go, and considering it started to drizzle. He's wearing a tweed jacket He's rather fond of and wouldn't want it damaged by the rain. Inside, a woman in her thirties, with an impressive dragon tattoo barely covered by a tank top, and a sleeping five-year-old girl.

He knows immediately He'd not derailed the *plan* whatever the plan is, only delayed it.

"My god, are you from the council? I've sent you lot the paperwork already. Bugger off, I've no time for this now."

The woman's name is Frankie, and Frankie is angry. The Devil thinks that if He were an inspector, He'd probably not look fondly on a child sleeping next to a mountain of colourful explosives, but He doesn't say that, because although He is the Devil, Frankie looks vaguely threatening, and He doesn't much like confrontation.

"I'm here to help you set up," He says instead, and she looks at His tweed jacket and slim hands doubtfully. It's not His fault, that He looks like an accountant or inspector, or professor of something like English Literature or Comparative Art History.

Frankie hands him boxes of something He needs to be very careful with, and He slowly walks them to a spot outside marked with a chalk X. She unpacks them, labels them, numbers them. The child doesn't stir.

Frankie doesn't get friendlier as the evening passes into night, but she does offer Him tea from her flask, and it tastes so much like Martha's He wants to cry, then wonders where that came from, that raw pain, but Frankie keeps her galaxy-brimming eyes on Him as if He were an imbecile, and so He tries to keep it together. The child cries out in her sleep, and He tries harder, because He knows it's His fault. He wonders if she were to wake up, would those same eyes be in her face, too.

Frankie mumbles about the decline of the town, and how much the council had fucked it. About the council flats, and council rooms in the Burstin, which is the ugliest building she had ever seen and *seriously, did none of those people have eyes?* The Devil remembers when it was still the Royal Pavilion, but He doesn't tell her that, or about the time Dickens came to stay. Instead He listens, as she becomes more and more vocal about the million little issues. It's been long since she had someone to listen. It smells like sewage at the harbour, after rain, she says. All the shops are shutting down, she says. Nobody has any money. The GP waiting list is four weeks, three if you're lucky.

It's no wonder people think the world is ending, the Devil thinks, but doesn't say that either.

People are congregating en masse on the Leas grass and pavement, around the band stand, an ocean of them to where the arc of the War Memorial proudly stands, and dozens of knitted poppies are clipped to the fence, each one a memory.

Frankie doesn't wake her daughter when the fireworks start, nor does she put on a coat. She's flushed with the cold, or maybe with exertion, or maybe with both. The Devil watches as colours explode in the sky. The same in France, across the water, and just as visible.

Four years later, Saga is sold and the De Haan Charitable Trust flourishes.

The world doesn't end.

****

In 2019, October, just before Halloween, the Devil comes through the Martello Tower no. 3 portal to Hell, and His heart sinks. The spiders are still there, and someone has been squatting inside. It's a good place to squat, as the walls are two and a half metres thick, and there is no way for elements to get to you, but He wonders what this means for the rest of the town.

Then He is at the Harbour Arm, and it's a Saturday, and there are bars and food and people everywhere, and although they complain about what they call "London prices" they're still there, buying pints of beer and mussels and something called "Iggy's Pop". Something loud and animated plays on the outdoor screen. The Devil walks up to the lighthouse and gets a glass of red. They don't want His coins, but luckily the tweed jacket He is still wearing produces a bank card which only need touch the reader to settle the transaction. He marvels at this, and at the phone which comes after the card. It's larger than the last one, but flat and cold to touch, with a screen with real colours, and BBC loads so fast He can't count the seconds.

The rest of the country seems to be in disarray, but here, life has elevated. There's still a way to go, but Folkestone no longer feels abandoned. Brexit is in progress, but now the Devil understands that no matter what year He comes in, something important will be happening.

He sits on a spindly, cast iron chair and looks to the water, smooth as a mirror. The tide is high, covering the small arches lining Sunny Sands, and people are swimming despite the cold. Back and forth, the small dot of a man moves across the water. He must be training for something, the Devil thinks, surely nobody would do this to themselves otherwise. The Tower stands in the middle of a golf course, a huge golden cornucopia between it and the sea. There is an orange cardboard-looking house floating inside the harbour, and the Devil feels perplexed by it, in a way that makes his wine taste sweeter because silly, strange, curious things like that mean life must be good.

The chair next to him is pulled away from the fence surrounding the harbour wall. A young woman sits on it but doesn't say "Is this seat taken?" as He'd expect her to, because she knows it isn't.

Her eyes have the sun in them, and the Devil knows that whatever had been in motion for the past two hundred years is now coming to be.

"You were there when the Tower was built." It's not a question. He answers *yes* anyway. "And at the train station." Not a question either.

She drinks a glass of something bubbly and faintly golden, looks surprised, the Devil notices that so does everyone else, and tempers His curiosity unsuccessfully. "Don't," she says, "tastes better this way."

The Devil realises He doesn't know her name, and it's the first time He remembers ever not knowing something. He's torn between asking for it and not asking, because although not knowing is suffocating and terrifying, it's also sweet and new. It's been a long time since He'd seen something new.

Finally, He gives in.

"It's Rebecca," she tells him. He tastes the name, repeats it after her. Rebecca has the voice of Luna, and the face of Martha, but also both of those are her own, and she's as forward as Frankie but as steady as Annabelle was as a baby.

She tells him it's a family story they've been telling for a long time, a man who appears out of nowhere and always the same except for his clothes. You can tell it's him, she says, because the air changes, and tea changes.

"Your family always gives me tea," he responds, not sure what else to say. They watch the man swim another lap.

Nothing happens on this day, or on this week. The Devil stays in Folkestone.

9

Lights Out on the Old High Street

by A L Marchant

It was a Wednesday.

My most disliked day of the week.

A nothing day

A nobody day.

A lonely day.

For whatever reason, the worst things that happened to me, happened on a Wednesday.

For whatever reason, all life drained from me on a Wednesday.

Bleakness swelled and Joy evaporated on a Wednesday.

To me, Wednesday is always a rainy day even when there is no rain.

It possesses within it that general attitude of being damp.

The kind of damp that gets trapped in the toe of your shoe after you mis-step into a puddle and never leaves.

It was a Wednesday.

And I was stuck with it for one more hour.

On this particular evening, at this specific hour, I felt particularly uninspired by it all.

The clock my mother gave me, which I used as a paperweight for scraps of receipts, seemed to tick louder than usual.

Abusively so.

There was nothing on television.

Infinite channels and a handful of streaming services, and the most I could do was tolerate a banal cooking show for five minutes, before an irrational hatred for everyone on the screen set

in, and I turned it off in disgust.

My stomach growled in frustration at me.

I'd spent half an hour thinking of what to have for dinner, before settling on some dull option, then

realising, once I'd started cooking, that I wasn't remotely hungry in the first place.

I sat, doing nothing, waiting for something.

Something never came.

I stood.

That did nothing to change the situation.

I paced.

In that moment I regretted Lenore no longer being there.

Not that I missed her.

It was just that I'd have liked to have seen her deal with the boredom too.

I thought of going to sleep.

But I couldn't.

My mind would not let me.

My mind can be a bastard at times.

I closed my eyes.

I sighed.

A deep sigh from the pit of my gut.

I heaved myself to my feet and lurched into my kitchen.

Hauling open my fridge door, my concerns were proved valid.

No food, apart from half a packet of cheese and a brown apple.

And worse, no booze.

Wednesday.

I considered the outside world.

I was wearing the shirt I had slept in.

I'd been wearing it all day.

It smelt of sleep still and felt as unwashed as I was.

I hadn't left the house in over 24 hours.

I needed air.

I felt strange, and I needed air.

Even if it was Wednesday air.

And so, with no plan, with nowhere to go, with nothing to do... I slipped on the ratty trainers I kept meaning to replace and left my trap of an apartment.

Instinctively, my feet found themselves walking towards town.

A route taken so often, that it took me a full minute to realise that I'd chosen where to go without thinking about it.

I knew nowhere would be open.

But that only added to the appeal, as I walked down dark streets, with only the occasional house illuminating a single window.

So, there I stood, in the centre of a ghost town.

Even the shops that hadn't closed were lifeless in this moment.

The town had gone to bed.

The town was done with Wednesday.

The town rested.

Nobody trod upon it at this moment, but me.

No oblivious masses swarming round one another transfixed at their phones.

No loudly rowing couples with their public displays of aggression.

No children terrorising seagulls with their stomping feet.

Not even any seagulls, come to that, waiting for the opportunity to steal half a sandwich.

Just the dark, the quiet, the town, and me.

Silence.

Stillness.

Then faintly, far off, the sound of a bottle breaking and possibly a couple arguing.

And with that, the night felt a little less still and I wished for the company I had just now enjoyed being absent

I decided to go to the sea.

My favourite route down to the beaches and the seafront was via the Old High Street.

A thin, quaint, cobbled stretch on a steepish hill.

An attempt to retain the feel of a yesterday town.

A road reclaimed by artists and entrepreneurs, full of eclectic wares and interesting eateries.

At the top sat the town, and at the bottom sat the sea - give or take a few turns.

It felt like a bridge - from one type of world to another.

Standing at the top of the road, looking down, I was surprised at the level of darkness.

I was certain I had come here at this time, or thereabouts, before, and that there had been streetlights.

What light I could see came from either the town behind me, the road at the bottom of the Old High Street, or the moon.

The street felt strange suddenly.

Less familiar.

Less warm.

It felt as if something was wrong.

Far off, but not so far as before, that hint of those rowdy voices sounded out again.

There was something fierce about how it sounded.

Feral almost.

I tried not to listen.

To not make out any words.

But the voices...

They were closer.

I brought the sea to the front of my mind.

Its calming roar, then hush, over and over.

That strange lullaby.

The beach in the darkness.

What a way to see in a new day.

Ignoring the voices, I began down the street.

Past galleries, past craftware, past cake shops.

Yet, the further I went, the dimmer these places seemed to become.

Or could I just have been getting tired, finally?

Past custom jewellery, past retro clothing.

Onward I went, down into the darkness.

Past the cafes of this steep street, past burger bars and t-shirt shops with bespoke designs.

Somehow, the end of the street seemed to be in absolute darkness.

Past paint shops and tapas bars and a place that usually smells of incense.

A smash behind me, a couple of loud voices laughing, swearing and jeering.

I cautiously looked behind me, trying to seem casual.

Trying to seem as if it were NOT my intention to look.

Trying to make it seem like something I just happened to do without any provocation.

I expected to see some lads perhaps.

Or perhaps a drunk couple with the same idea as me of a midnight trip to the beach.

I almost expected a clown, jeering at me in the night.

Something...

But there was nothing.

Just the top of the street.

And nothing else...

Then suddenly voices came, loud, overlapping, shrieking over the top of each other, crude, raucous, terrifying, and my heart leapt into my throat, since they were undeniably coming from where I was looking...

Where nobody was...

Apart from a growing shadow.

I refused to believe what I was experiencing.

Yet the noise just grew and became overwhelming.

There must have been ten, maybe twenty voices.

It was impossible to be sure.

I let out the smallest yelp of alarm.

And then they were silent.

And it felt as if dozens of eyes that I could not see had turned to look around at me.

I fixed MY eyes to where the bottom of the street should be, and began to walk briskly, turned myself, determined to leave the Old High Street as quickly as I could.

But the bottom of the street was nothing but blackness.

It was so dark that not one thing could be made out.

No greeting card shops, no movie memorabilia shops, no kids' clothing shops.

None of those safe havens could be seen.

There was just the complete absence of all.

I took some steps, past where a tattoo parlour should be.

Past where record or camera shops should be.

Past where that lovely little shop with those cute little things in the window should be.

On into nothingness.

And I started to dread there may not even be an end to this street anymore.

Behind me the voices began again.

In a whisper at first.

One or two.

Then louder.

Four or five.

Then louder.

Ten. Twelve.

I walked faster, trying to negotiate both the cobbles and the dip in the street with my useless, useless, worn out shoes.

The voices were right behind me.

Words indistinct, but a tone of definite hostility.

Or maybe that was how I imagined it.

But I had to get away.

Tears welled in my eyes.

I tried to control my fear.

It felt like the darkness all around was reaching out with shadowy tendrils.

I felt a breath on the back of my neck, and I yelled in alarm, running for all of two steps before tripping on an unseeable curb and landing flat on my face in the shape of a shop doorway.

And the darkness consumed me.

The next thing I knew, the side of my face burned, and my mouth tasted like iron as it filled with blood.

I blinked and the world seemed literally brighter.

The moon had returned, having vanished without me noticing.

The light from either end of the Old High Street had returned.

And there WERE streetlights here.

And the voices...

They seemed to be gone.

I got to my feet and staggered - stumbled downwards, leaning on walls or windows whenever I needed to.

More often than I'd have liked.

Finally, I had escaped...

My mind could not process what had just happened.

It was too relieved as I stepped off the cobbles and heard the call of the sea.

And with it...

Ever so faintly...

Voices.

Loud.

Raucous.

Many.

Whether they were the voices I had just been terrorised by, or completely normal, high spirited human voices, I could not tell.

And I would not find out.

I turned from the sea and went home.

Wednesdays.

Once I got home, once I took off my shoes and cleaned my teeth, spat out the blood, found some paracetamol under the sofa and stood staring at my unmade bed, I realised...

I could not bring myself to turn off the light.

I could not bring myself to embrace the dark after all I had experienced.

And what had I experienced?

What had happened?

Was it in my mind?

Was it real?

Was it tied to the night?

Or the town?

Or that strange, enchanting street that I loved so much?

Could I ever experience any of those things again without being triggered into reliving the events of this night?

I spent the rest of the night in my armchair, staring out of the window with the light on.

I sat there until the sun rose over the row of houses across from mine.

And once the sun rose, I slept.

It was a Thursday.

10

A Necessary Witness

by

Tony Hulse

The house stands alone, perilously close to the edge of soaring sea cliffs. It is reached by a rough track that slopes slightly upward as it struggles toward the forlorn stone gateposts, a void where once was ornate iron flower and leaf: "Sea View."

It is known by locals as "The White House" although that title seems strangely inappropriate – considering its disturbing history. Perhaps, long ago, it was "white", in the sense of being pure or at peace. Now it seems to have the pallor of the shroud, the grey off-white of death. As it fades in and out of the cloying sea mists that plague this coast, it could seem to the casual passer-by that it was trying to hide itself from prying eyes or inquisitive minds.

The large garden at the front appears unloved, neglected. The central focus is the fountain, weathered granite, and shallow, stagnant water in its trio of shell-shaped basins. A cherub eternally inhabits the centre, standing, hands clasped in prayer, face turned imploringly to the heavens. There is something unnerving about it – both the hollow eye sockets, and the rather chilling idea that someone might create a seraph designed to endlessly cry.

To add to the sense of decay, the rose bushes in the borders either side of the wide front steps have grown wild. A struggle of thorns and petals, pinks and yellows constantly browning in the damp, briny air.

The huge Georgian sash-windows seem particularly unwelcoming in that the glass appears opaque, possessing a quick-silver sheen that reflects the hastily passing clouds with an almost cinematic resonance.

This reluctance continues with the panelled wooden door; the absence of knocker or bell testifies to no desire for visitors. The royal blue is almost black beneath years of grime. Carved into the lintel is the disheartening image of a schooner in the intimate, deadly embrace of some colossal sea serpent. It could perhaps, to those of a sensitive nature, appear like a warning.

At the back, however, one could almost begin to imagine that it might be a pleasant enough place to live. Tall French windows open on to a wide, south-facing patio with uninterrupted views of the English Channel and the coast of France beyond. Either side of the doors are comfortable, high-backed wooden benches, placed no doubt to provide a vantage point for observing the constant traffic of Dover ferries, or the leisurely sails of summer.

Although the central path is still visible, long grasses and obstinate thistles have overrun the lawns that descend towards the low, balustraded wall that literally rounds off the safety of the gardens from the tussocky, crumbling peril of the cliff edge. Yes, once it may have been a desirable abode. But houses, like people, are shaped by their past and "Sea View" had seen the worst of human weakness and cruelty.

It is not quite six months since the November day that saw my first visit to the house on the cliff. It seems so much longer, like looking back at a different world, the fiction of someone else's life.

It was just getting dark as I returned to the welcome warmth of our high street branch. In truth, it was one of those cold, grey, monotonous days when it never really seems to get light. This, combined with a mild hangover from last night's bonfire party, may have been partly to blame for my unusual melancholy. I was also vaguely aware of a nagging sense of unease. I remember Dan, all spiky hair and spiky charm, was there, on his mobile, talking to a customer. He was just twenty, twelve years younger than me, and annoyingly enthusiastic and arrogant in equal measure.

I sat at my computer and tried to shut out his banter as I uploaded my photos and started to type, flexing the cold out of my chilled fingers.

"Unique, detached Victorian house with fine views of the English Channel."

I sat back in my swivel chair and sighed. Uninspired, clichéd, and bland - but worse still, dishonest. "Unique"? Unsettling more like. "Detached"? Exposed would be more appropriate. Dan interrupted my musings.

"You alright Matt?"

"Yeah yeah – just trying to write-up that new instruction in Capel"

"What, that creepy place up on the cliff?"

I paused for a moment. I did not want to encourage him. I was feeling intolerant and adverse to any small talk.

"Not creepy as such. Just a bit bleak."

Dan shrugged, lost interest, looking at his watch as he wheeled back in his chair.

"Right, I'm gone – viewing at five. Tell Wardo I'll see him tomorrow!"

I waved in his direction and carried on staring at the screen.

The photographs were no use at all. I had hoped the house would look somehow grand against the leaden skies, but the banks of cloud seemed to overwhelm it. The "money shot" – the view over to France – was even worse. The sea was lost in the murk and further obscured by a dark "smudge" right of centre. My thumb I presumed. I muttered to myself and continued my doomed efforts to enthuse about "Sea View"

It was just after five-thirty when "Wardo" – Alan Ward – arrived back. As a young man he would have appeared driven, determined. Now, in middle-age, he appeared more frustrated and disillusioned. His deliberately extravagant sideburns and ruddy complexion gave him an almost Edwardian air which was not dispelled by his slightly too large tweed jacket. He was typically to the point.

"How'd you get on at Capel?"

I shared my disappointment and showed him the photos.

"What is that?"

He pointed at the shot taken from the patio. The black mark had somehow spread, appearing more mottled as it covered the screen, like a lace veil had been placed across the lens. Just a corner of the wall was still visible.

"I've told you before, use the SLR. I've told you both – phones are for phoning!"

He sounded irritated – and weary.

"I'll go up there again as soon as the weather improves," I offered.

"As soon as... there's a lot riding on this one. Been on with three previous agents in the past two years. We'd be looking at two percent of close to a million."

"Two years? Won't anyone stump up the mortgage?"

He grunted. "No problem with finance... just superstitious nonsense..."

His annoyance stopped me from enquiring further.

"Can you lock up, Matthew? I've got a bloody Rotary Club do."

He waved half-heartedly over his shoulder as he opened the door. I felt the rush of night air and shivered involuntarily. "Night, Alan" I called out as he slammed it shut.

It was almost a week before the weather made any significant improvement. I drove the scenic route out of town, around the East Cliff, past the pavilion with its Italian style clock tower, up the gentle curve of Wear Bay Road. It was remarkably calm for Autumn and the sun simmered silver on the slight swell. Looking up and along towards Dover, my destination was clearly visible, imperious and benign in the fresh morning light.

It felt good to be outside. A warm October had delayed the inevitable and so here we were, in mid-November, still enjoying nature's rich prologue to winter. It was also good to get away from the office. Dan had been commenting for days about the dire quality of my "Sea View" photographs. He compounded this puerile teasing by narrating some far-fetched tale about the property's sinister past and "The Grey Lady" he had heard about in some drunken conversation in the British Lion.

I'd decided to try and impress Alan with a little creativity. I wanted to get some shots of the house from sea level, far below, to establish the magnificence of its setting. Consequently, my first stop was the Cliff Top Cafe car park from where a footpath meandered downwards. I pulled up on the gravel next to a sole Nissan Micra. Dog walkers, I presumed, this early on a Wednesday with the cafe being closed. I confess my mood was enhanced even further by the contrast of BMW and salmon-pink mini. I am self-aware enough to recognise my acquisitive side and the constant, materialist need to satiate it.

The view from here, back towards Folkestone was always impressive, but particularly so on a day such as this. The town nestling compactly behind the harbour seemed infused in a golden haze and the curve of the coast right round to Dungeness Point was delightfully articulate.

I got my rucksack and a bottle of water from the back seat and headed for the steps down to the top of the path. I looked below to where it wound through the trees to the area of landslip and under-cliff known as The Warren. Beyond the woods, I could see the railway, and the foot bridge over it, which was my destination.

I began my descent rather carefully, the chalk still slippery from recent rains, and uneven in places. My theory about dog walkers was confirmed halfway down by the approach of a slightly breathless middle-aged couple and their boisterous Scottie.

"Morning" they both observed. "Beautiful day."

This cheerful, sociable exchange lifted my spirits all the further. Strange how life is. The happiness and contentment we strive for arrives unannounced and is then, just as unexpectedly, snatched away.

I continued downwards until I reached the path through the wood that eventually led to the bridge. I looked up, to the right. I still couldn't see the house, but the light-blue wash of sky through the greens and reds of the canopy boded well for my low-angle "establishing" shot.

There was no-one else around. Unseen birds were pipetting close-by and further away the chattering of a single magpie. I stood and listened. Out at sea the diesel chug of a trawler faded Folkestone-wards.

I began striding purposefully along the path which undulated through vivid green ferns and bramble beds. As a child I had imagined dinosaurs down here, the semi-unfurled ferns seeming somehow prehistoric. After about five minutes, I came out of the trees and stopped to have a drink. As I unscrewed the cap, I glanced back up towards Sea View. The house was visible again now, but it was not this that I was focused on.

Standing motionless, virtually on the very edge of the cliff was a slight, silhouetted figure. I think I spoke aloud – "What is she doing?" I had immediately assumed it was a woman from the cut and the fall of her clothes, though they were indistinct, dark. It was impossible at this distance to make out her face, particularly as she appeared to be hooded

Looking back, I think my first reaction was that plunging, clutching sensation of dread that seizes you when you realise something terrible is about to occur – the car in front spinning out of control, the drunken thugs crossing the street towards you. That initial emotion was, however, short lived

As I stared, unsure whether to call out or phone for help, I experienced something truly original, unknown to me in my thirty-two cynical, sceptical years. It was primeval, timeless, borne of a horror conjured by fear of the unknown, the unfathomable, the unexplained. She had started to wave.

It seems innocuous enough as I write it now, but it haunts me still and plagues my dreams. Although she remained rooted to the spot, she had lifted her right arm and was moving it slowly in a rigid arc starting in front of her hidden face, then high above her head, and then out to the side, then back, then again, back, then again. It was so exaggerated, so intense that I turned to look out to sea half expecting to see who or what she was waving at. Nothing – even the trawler had found harbour. That said, I realised that I could now only see out a few hundred yards. Beyond that a turbid wall of fog was moving slowly coast wards across the stilled, mercurial waters. I turned back and looked up. She still stood there, but she had stopped waving. She was motionless again, but with her arms extended out in front, palms facing upwards, as though beckoning.

I'd seen enough. I pulled my bag off my back and fumbled in the side pocket for my phone. No signal. Why did I think there would be? She remained, in the same uncanny pose, inches back from sheer, certain death.

I raced stumbling, ungainly, back through the woods. It was much darker now, the mist was wiping and rolling up the cliffs and the sun was virtually obscured. The temperature was dropping sharply and yet I was sweating as I began to climb. Halfway up I stopped to catch my breath. I checked my phone again – still no signal. I could see little above or below. It was just as I started forward again, I heard the most awful sound. The disorientating mire made it hard to place; it seemed inexplicably close, almost immediately above. Unmistakeably, a desperate, shrill, woman's scream that became a word, a word that reverberated several times in a drawn-out, agonising wail – "No!" And then the unmistakeable sound of someone falling, crying out as air became unyielding rock, became snapping, crashing branch.

I found myself leaning against the cold metal handrail, clinging on, shaking uncontrollably. It was several minutes before I felt I could move. I don't really remember reaching the top or getting into my car. Eventually, I looked at my mobile. I had a signal. My hand was still shaking as I tapped, 999. Emergency services! I could have phoned before! "Stupid, stupid..." I punched my left fist against the dashboard. I could have saved her.

It took me two whole days to realise the truth. That I was not the knight in shining armour, no saviour; that I was merely a necessary witness, a defender of truth against injustice.

There was of course no body found, no broken trees, no sign of a fall. I phoned in sick on Thursday and spent the day in bed sleeping fitfully and briefly.

On the Friday I went to the local library (my laptop was at the office) and started to research "The Grey Lady, Capel."

A local history site had details of Kent hauntings. The "legend" was that Carlotta Iniesta was a Spanish born servant girl. She had worked for the family in the "big house" on the cliff. There was an eldest son, aged twenty. They had become lovers, but then the parents had sent him away to "university" in Paris. He had promised Carlotta he would return. However, the parents had other ideas. They invented stories about his previous philandering. Still she would not give him up, each day staring obsessively out to sea at approaching ships. So, they concocted a letter, had it sent from France. Simple and brutal. He had never loved her; she should return to Spain and so forth. Carlotta chose another way, straight down, 300 feet. It was only when they found her broken body that they realised she was "with child."

That should have been that. I decided I would tell nobody – I didn't think anyone would believe me anyway. On the Monday I shrugged off Alan's questions about where I had got to on the Wednesday before. I light-heartedly suggested I was not the man for the Sea View job – the weather seemed to be against me! So, Alan "gave it" to Dan (who grinned smugly, I recall). That should have been that. But, of course, it wasn't.

Christmas came and went. Work was typically "quiet" for the time of year. Alan set us new, unreachable targets. On the surface all seemed as before. I drank lots of coffee to cover my lack of sleep (each night the same dream – the desperate wind milling wave, the wretched scream). I hardly registered Dan's change of mood. "I'm fine – domestics" he'd say when I'd enquire about his dark stubble or his lack of conversation.

And then, yesterday. I had arrived at the office feeling slightly more optimistic; I had slept right through and there were signs of spring abundant in the ebullient daffodils that lined my route into work.

Dan went out early, and about mid-morning, Alan left for a meeting at the bank. I had not been alone for long when the phone rang. It was Lucy, Dan's girlfriend of some two years. Nineteen, blond, out of college and out of work.

"Hi Matt. Is Dan there?"

I told her he was out. She did not respond immediately.

"Could you ask him to call me please?" She sounded upset.

"Are you alright, Luce?"

"No – not really. He's left me Matt... Walked out three weeks ago" And then, more quietly, "I'm pregnant. I'm having his baby."

I put the phone down and sat back. Almost immediately it rang again. Mrs Armstrong. Dan was meant to be there at 10-00 for a valuation. He hadn't shown. I told her I would contact him and get back to her. I rang his mobile. No answer. It didn't even cut to voice mail. With a growing sense of unease, I crossed to his desk and opened his diary. March 18th. There were no appointments listed, no client details, just a single, elaborate doodle. A sinuous heart-shape around a single initial, his initial, "D". But it was written backwards. And then the gradual realisation, the icy shiver. The "heart", on closer examination, was a ghastly, contorting sea serpent and the backward D was no such thing – it was the initials "C" and "I", written close together.

My actions became almost impulsive. I locked-up, not even bothering with a "Back soon" sign. I raced through amber lights on Cherry Garden Road, almost lost control at seventy on the sharp bend on Dover Hill. The day was still clear, just the occasional fair-weather cloud and as I sped along the New Dover Road, I could see Sea View, distinct, apart, remote. And the helicopter hovering and whirring just above the cliffs. As I turned right, up the track, I knew.

Dan's VW was parked just inside the gates, as were police cars, an ambulance, and a fire engine. I reversed back, parked on the track, and jumped out. I hurried around the back of the house. A number of police and men wearing high visibility vests were standing or kneeling on the cliff edge. I felt my head spin, thought for a moment I would faint.

It was then I noticed a familiar face, sitting on one of the benches. The woman dog walker and her irrepressible Scottie. She had clearly been crying and was gripping a sodden tissue tightly in her hand alongside the dog's lead. I walked slowly over and sat down. The dog stood and wagged its tail, mercifully oblivious. She smiled in recognition.

"Are you ok?" was all I could offer.

She looked at me and I could see the horror in her wide eyes.

"I saw him... I saw him. I was back along there, on the cliff path. He was at the bottom of the garden and then he stepped over the wall and..." She stopped, put her hand to her face. "He started walking towards the edge. He was holding his hands out in front - like this" She stretched out her left arm, the palm facing upwards. "I called out, but he just kept walking, towards the edge... he seemed to reach out and then..." She stopped as the words failed her. I touched her arm.

"He didn't even cry out," she said quietly, almost to herself.

I do not know how long I sat there. Eventually, spurred on by the policeman who wanted a statement from my companion, I wandered back round to the front. Another car – a coastguard had arrived and several people in uniforms were standing around talking quietly. I was dazed, but also confused. Something was different – a sound.

I turned my head, towards the centre of the garden where the fountain stood, melancholy as before. But now, it had trickled into life, and with a splutter, and a gurgle, the "tears" began to splash into the waiting basins. With a supreme effort of will, I fought the rush of darkness, turned, and walked out of the gates, never to return.

11

The Thirsty Librarian

by Mark Brophy

Thomas felt rough. His head hurt and his hands were shaking more than usual. As he dragged his bad leg along the dusty, sun-drenched summer streets of Folkestone, he could think of nothing but his undying thirst. He was always thirsty, and the heat of the noonday sun was not helping matters. He had risen late that day, his nightmares had kept him awake for most of the moonless night and he'd spent the morning drifting in and out of sleep. Thomas was unable to forget the scenes he had witnessed in 1914 when German forces had brought war to the place of his birth, the town of Louvain, Belgium.

He had been happy there and had found true contentment working amongst a rich variety of books housed at the Catholic university library. In fact, Thomas had become obsessed with words from an early age and he loved nothing more than to be surrounded by great works, preferring reading to any social communication. The library contained hundreds of rare texts and manuscripts and as Thomas worked conscientiously on a particularly difficult translation, the thought that this precious place could be destroyed never entered his head.

German forces had crossed the border into Belgium some weeks before, as what was to become known as World War 1 broke out. Liege had succumbed to German military might and Louvain itself was already occupied. Within the confines of the library walls, life had continued normally, shielded from events outside. Thomas buried himself in his work which he felt to be extremely important. Noise from outside disturbed him as he tried to concentrate, gunfire ringing out across the courtyard. He was annoyed at the interruption and clenched his teeth as the door to his chamber was flung open.

"Come on! We must flee!" cried Thomas' long-time friend, Edgar, who stood in the doorway with terror in his eyes.

"I'm not going anywhere," asserted Thomas. "I need to finish this text," he said without looking up. Edgar walked over and placed his hand on Thomas's shoulder. He knew commanding Thomas would never work, but gentle persuasion might.

"We must go, Thomas. Put the translation in your bag if you must, but if we remain, it will be the last translation you ever do."

Reluctantly, Thomas packed the books into his satchel as Edgar urged him to hurry. Shouts could be heard nearby as people began to flee and the walls of the town began to quake. As the two friends made their way downstairs into the depths of the library, Thomas smelled the unmistakable scent of petrol. Within minutes, the building was alight, and fire ripped through the reading rooms. A soot like dust fell from the rafters as falling masonry broke through the roof. The two men hurried to the entrance of a concealed passageway and the ancient tunnel that led downwards into the dark, their only chance of escape.

Above, all hell was breaking loose as the battle of Louvain began, the noise slowly fading away thanks to the thick insulating earth above. After over an hour traversing the narrow, claustrophobic tunnel, they emerged into the warm night air. The sounds of war were again loud in their ears as they scrambled onto the dusty earth. The sky was bright with flames which spread like wildfire through small wooden houses and close-knit streets. As they reached the edge of town, a loud boom rang out. The friends watched in horror as a huge shell struck the bell tower of the library, bringing the whole roof down and shrouding the beautiful architecture in smoke and dust. The bell tumbled to the ground ringing out of tune as it fell. In a couple of days, Louvain would be reduced to smouldering rubble.

The two men realised their lives would never be the same again and resolved to head for the relative safety of France. They journeyed across the land ahead of the approaching German forces and joined the masses of refugees seeking safety. The kindness of strangers saved Thomas and Edgar as they were given shelter and sustenance as they travelled. Their adventures are too numerous to tell here, suffice to say that through luck and determination, the pair of them reached the shores of the French coast.

Thomas and Edgar, being unsuitable for front line service, became nurses. Initially they worked to guide thousands of refugees onto boats bound for Britain. As the war intensified, they helped countless victims of trench warfare in the field hospitals of France and became heroes to the people they saved. Unfortunately, Edgar became sick himself and it was decided that he should be taken to the military hospital at Shorncliffe, near Folkestone. Thomas also was soon relieved of his duties, increasingly unable to walk due to an old leg injury. And so, it was that the two friends left the shores of mainland Europe in 1917.

The sea was calm as the hospital ship slid out of port and a quiet anticipation pervaded the decks. It wouldn't take long to cross the channel and while Thomas breathed in the still dusk air, the faint sound of shelling could be heard in the distance. Thomas felt guilty to be leaving for a safer shore though the journey across this short stretch of water was notoriously dangerous. He leant over the side peering into the dark glistening water. He looked out towards the English coast and could just make out the chalkiness of the white cliffs, faintly visible in the half-light. Then he noticed something unusual in the sea - a white streak formed by something speeding under the surface. With horror he realised what it was.

"T-t-t-t-t-torpedo!" he stuttered.

"Torpedo!!!" he shouted as loudly as his terrified lungs allowed.

But it was too late, the torpedo struck the ship with a deafening boom!

And that was as much as Thomas could remember. He couldn't remember fighting for his life in the flame-infested sea after the torpedo struck or the desperate swim to the rescue boat. He didn't remember his rescuers or the hours of nursing that kept him alive, but one thing he was certain of was that Edgar must have surely perished. And so it was that Thomas found himself on the hot summer streets of Folkestone feeling a thirst like never before.

He walked up Church Slope from the harbour, the steep cobbled road paining his leg. He was making for a bar, any bar to soothe his cares away and numb the pain. He was strangely drawn to Sandgate Road where he noticed an open door and some steps leading downwards. He descended as fast as his leg would allow. He pushed on the heavy wooden doors at the bottom and found himself in a large chamber with tables, comfortable chairs and a warm glow from the candlelit walls. He made his way to the counter. There was nothing on display, nothing to say what they sold and no price list or menu.

"What'll it be, Sir?" asked the barmaid.

"What can you offer?" quizzed Thomas.

"Anything your heart desires," the lady returned.

"How can you offer anything? There's a war on you know. You shouldn't be so cruel as to offer anything."

"There's no war on in here," the lady replied curtly, "Now what'll it be?" Thomas frowned. "Ok. A real Belgian beer," he said, challenging the lady at a game he knew she couldn't win.

"There you are," she said, presenting Thomas with a foaming flagon of ale. He took several large gulps at what was the most satisfying beer he had ever had. The lady turned away as he reached for his wallet.

"What about payment, young lady?" he asked.

"It's on the house," she said, as she turned back smiling.

Thomas stood dumbfounded. He took a sip. Wow! It tasted amazing! He shuffled over to a table and sat down, noticing somebody else just coming in through the heavy doors.

"What'll it be?" he heard the lady say once again.

"Cognac I think today please," said a familiar voice.

"Where do I know that voice from?" thought Thomas. Then he remembered with a shiver, it was very much like Edgar's voice. Strange too because his dearest friend had been partial to Cognac.

Thomas turned to look and saw a smartly dressed man. A man who would not look out of place working in a university library! Thomas nearly fell off his chair - it *was* Edgar! Overjoyed, he stood up with tears running down his face.

Edgar turned and beamed at Thomas.

"Hello old friend," Edgar said, and Thomas realised he looked somehow younger and fitter than when he last saw him. They shook hands warmly as Thomas studied the face of his old friend.

"I have to ask; how did you manage to survive the torpedo attack?" Thomas said as they sat at the table.

"I didn't," replied Edgar without blinking.

“What do you mean? How come you are here now, sat before me?” “Well, you see, I’m dead. I mean, I’m a ghost. Funny thing is, you are too.” Thomas was stunned into silence.

“Look around, nobody in here is alive - it’s a ghost only bar,” laughed Edgar with a broad smile. “But don’t worry, being a ghost does have some benefits.” Thomas couldn’t believe his ears. He was speechless.

Laughing at Thomas’ confusion, Edgar went on to explain.

“When you die, someone volunteers to guide you into the spirit world. I wanted to be your guide, so here I am.” Edgar grinned broadly again.

It was hard to believe, but in a strange way it made sense and explained how little he actually remembered. When he had awoken that day, he had acted almost without thinking, walking as if compelled in some way. Now in this bar sitting with Edgar, a peace came over him. For the first time in years, his leg no longer hurt, and his headache had gone.

“The worst thing,” continued Edgar, “is the thirst. You never quite get rid of that thirst. Fancy another?”

Thomas grinned.

“Why not? Especially if they’re on the house!”

12

This is my house

by Deborah J Jones

Impervious to disapproving looks, invincible in her sleek red 4x4 with blacked-out windows, Susi Ainsboro was parked on the zigzag lines outside the school, waving fondly at her children, winding the window down so she could blow them a kiss. She drove off erratically, almost taking out a mother with a large pram holding a little boy by the hand. Dowdy old bat. Who carted their children around in a contraption like that these days anyway? She had everything now – the car and the big house, grander than anything she and her husband could have afforded in London. They had worked hard over the summer, uncovering the original features, stripping back floorboards and restoring the Victorian mosaic of tiles at the top of the steps. All part of a carefully constructed life. Even her name was distinctive, spelt with an "I" with no "e" to follow. She sang along happily to the radio as she drove along Bouverie Road West. Home first, then a quick wander around the shops before a session at the gym; she found it difficult to find enough to occupy her days. She screamed as she felt a thud and a flash of colour swept across her field of vision.

Edith Lawrence, a few moments before, had been ensconced in her comfortable seat in the window at the Hideaway, its purple velour complementing her immaculate purple two piece. She was admiring a money plant in an attractive ceramic pot. The kindly young man behind the counter – his name was Matthew, she had learnt – came over from time to time to ask if she wanted anything, but she always declined, politely. He worked too hard, she thought; so did his wife. To Edith, this wasn't a hideaway. To her, it would always be Percy Webb's Grocery, purveyor of the finest coffees, teas and the best bacon in Folkestone.

She had been Mr Webb's shop girl. She could – probably should - as her mother had remarked, have done better for herself, but their circumstances had changed. She had needed the work and the shop was a stone's throw from their home. The Webb girls had grown up and married – handsome young men from the army camp. Edith had stayed on, enjoying the bustle and the warmth, and the banter with customers. She was enjoying it now. The ornate till had long gone, as had the cash carrier the Webbs had installed, to transfer money hygienically from customer to shop assistant, but the atmosphere was the same. If she closed her eyes, she could picture the delivery boy, setting off on his rounds, basket perched precariously on the crossbar of his bicycle. And herself, stepping out with a little hamper of muscatel raisins and almonds for the local hospital raffle. Mr Webb had always supported the local community generously. Matthew was just the same. Speaking of "rounds," it was time to make a move. She waved to Matthew as she slipped out of the door and he waved back. The customer he was serving looked round curiously, but Edith had gone.

Ponytail bobbing indignantly, as if to lend emphasis to each word, Susi leaned out of the window and shouted: "Stupid old cow." The London inflection had crept back in, which her husband always insisted she should curb in herself and correct in the children. "Why don't you look where you're going? Should be in a home at your age. Bloody liability."

Pulling into a nearby parking space, she climbed down. Edith was already on her feet. She would have driven off - felt like doing so - but there were a few people around and it would be just her luck...

"Are you all right?" Susi asked, grudgingly.

"I'm fine, dear," Edith replied. "I'll be right as rain after a sit down."

Feeling uncharacteristically abashed, Susi offered to drive Edith home. "The car's right there." "Yes, it's rather difficult to miss." Edith smiled. "No thank you, dear, I'll walk. I live just around the corner – Ingles Road."

She had a couple of hours in the parking bay, what the hell! "Oh, that's where I live. I'll walk with you."

"Just here." Edith indicated a turning. "Past the Turkish Baths. Father used to work there, before the war."

Susi's head was spinning. "Turkish Baths?" She hadn't heard of any such thing. She resolved to ask at the gym. Away with her thoughts, she was startled to see that Edith was already at the top of the steps, on her lovingly restored mosaic tiles, beside the front door with its tasteful stained glass.

"Well, this is my house. Goodbye dear."

Susi blinked. Edith had gone. She cursed, realising her handbag – with her keys and mobile- was still on the backseat. She hammered on the door, but there was no reply. She peered through the letterbox and shouted obscenities through it. Nobody came. She and her husband had already fallen out with the neighbours- it hadn't taken long – over parking and the building works – so nobody had a spare key. Giving the door one last kick with the toe of her fur-lined boot, she turned and retraced her steps.

"Good riddance," Edith murmured. She gave the rocking horse in the hall a friendly pat. How she would have loved one as a child, but life had changed after her father's death from dysentery in German custody. It had taken the War Office months to confirm what had happened and to issue her mother with a grudging, paltry pension. The house had been a boarding house, but she and her mother had scraped enough money together to buy it, for a song, when their landlady passed away. She drifted happily through the rooms, exclaiming to herself over some of the alterations but glad to note that the big marble fireplace was still there.

Susi wandered into the Hideaway, in need of a coffee and - sod the calories - something sweet. She liked it in there, always a friendly welcome.

"Hope you don't mind my saying," Matthew interrupted her reverie. "You look pale, as if you've seen a ghost."

He listened thoughtfully as, in between mouthfuls of carrot cake, Susi explained what had happened and about the old lady who had somehow got into the house, although she was sure she had locked the door before embarking on the school run.

"That sounds like Edith. She comes in every day. She was run over in the sixties. Don't worry, she's friendly. Well, I've always found her so. Used to work here and lived in Ingles Road."

He realised he was talking to himself – people might say he was making a habit of it – as Susi was already halfway down the road and clawing at the door of her 4x4.

Only a few days later, Susi's husband waved the removal man off – Susi had refused point blank to return to the house – and locked the door. An expensive little exercise, he thought bitterly. Well, he had had just about enough of her. She could stay at her mother's, for all he cared, or better still, go to hell.

Edith stood at the window on the top floor. It was her bedroom, not a playroom. She hoped the next people would be more congenial. She raised her hand in farewell, but the 4x4 had already disappeared around the corner.

13

Mystery of Lost Ben Wheeler

by Jana Chatters

Going back about a hundred years, the coastal town of Folkestone was one of the most popular seaside places in Britain. As befitted a holiday destination for royalty, it boasted fashionable hotels, coffee rooms, parks and other stylish buildings. But without the financial support of Earl Radnor and an active Folkestone Corporation we certainly wouldn't be able to appreciate the pride of the South Kent Coast these days.

In 1918 Folkestone Council made a decision to start a reconstruction project within two years. At the start of the year 1920, local people would have noticed an unusual hustle and activity along the Leas, on the steep slope. Before they could learn what was happening, they frowned at what might become of their comfortable walking path with its sea view. Regardless, the new Zig Zag path was started as access from the coast to the Leas, enhanced with artificial caves.

For a number of unemployed men, it was good news. For the London building Company of Mr. R.J. Pulham, it was not difficult to get enough workers for the project. In June, when building work started, the area looked like an anthill. Workers came from all the villages around Folkestone by foot, or by horse and carriage, keen to earn money. One of them, Tony Wheeler from Cheriton, had a wife and five children. He had to get up daily at four in the morning, to get to his work place on time. Labouring work, digging the steep and rocky ground, he managed with ease and enthusiasm, without having to pause for rest.

"You're a really good chap!" he would hear people say behind his back. The foreman, who stood nearby, praised him and patted Tony on the shoulder. After a short conversation, the foreman agreed to take on Tony's older son Ed, for casual work. Delighted, Tony thanked the foreman many times and looked forward to sharing the happy news with his family. The youngest child, Ben, who was five, listened eagerly to his father's speech and was more and more keen to see this unusual building work and the town of Folkestone, where he had been only once before – to the doctor's, as a toddler. A few days later, when his father had finished his dinner, Ben sat near him and started begging: "Dad, could you take me with you to Folkestone? I'd really like to see the building work. I'll sit on the green close to you and Ed and watch you all."

After two days, Mr Wheeler managed to secure a lift for the three of them to Folkestone, on a horse and cart. He put their belongings and food on the green by a lamppost, near their work place.

"See Ben, here's the spot where we'll have lunch at one o'clock. Don't go too far away so I can call you and see you!" The boy was nodding, but at the same time staring around at the rush and noise, and the large number of workers and equipment, the likes of which he had never seen before. Once his father had left with his older brother, Ben enjoyed looking round the building site tremendously. He wasn't quite sure what to look at first, but his observation was unexpectedly interrupted.

"Hi, what are you doing here?" A boy about his age stood in front of him. His name was Andy. He was local and was there for the same reason as Ben.

"My father is over there!" Andy pointed in the direction of a group of workers nearby. Both boys were enjoying themselves now, as they chatted and laughed.

Later, Ben's father was very happy, when all three sat on the green and had lunch together. Ben chatted happily about his new-found friend. He assured his father that he would be back before four o'clock, as Andy's father had a watch with him.

A few minutes after four, as Ed collected their belongings together, Tony Wheeler started looking around to find Ben. They walked around the building site desperately calling "B-e-n" at the top of their voices. They were grateful to get help from the foreman, who offered to call the Police. After more than two hours searching, the policeman recommended that both men went home, with the promise that he would continue searching and if he found Ben, he would keep him at the Police Station overnight.

Mrs Wheeler was distraught at the news . Her husband tried to calm her, but they – and Ed – had a long, sleepless, uncomfortable night. Only their three other children, who had no idea about their parents' worry, slept properly.

Next morning, Mr Wheeler and Ed arrived back at work. They frantically looked around, calling Ben down the slope, until a policeman appeared. He assured them that the search for Ben had continued until late the previous night and they would carry on again today, using a police dog this time.

"I am sure he wouldn't go near the sea! He is afraid of water, I am sure!" Tony repeated this sentence several times, with tears in his eyes.

For the first time in months, Tony's shift was more torment than work he liked. Both father and son looked around and instead of taking a lunch break walked along the Leas up and down to the coast.

Four days with no trace of Ben. Four evenings of returning home with no news. Mrs Wheeler became paler than ever and couldn't eat. They could do nothing to calm her down.

Meanwhile rumours started to circulate in Folkestone, spread by some of the local people who had been enjoying evening walks along The Leas. Many reported having heard soft and muted crying, a child's voice, coming from the coastal area. Nobody dared to go through the building site, or look at the new artificial caves, which had just started to appear. Some people believed they could hear the cries in other hidden places in the town.

One morning, when Tony and Ed arrived for work, they dropped their belongings in the same place as usual and looked around with sadness in their eyes. Tony couldn't summon the strength to call Ben any more.

"Mr Wheeler! Tony! Are you there?" They could hear shouts from some men nearby. They noticed a group of workers dashing from a westerly direction along The Leas. Around them a dog was jumping and in the middle of the crowd he could see a policeman carrying a bundle. At first, Tony froze, but he suddenly took off rapidly heading towards the group. He recognised the bundle in the policeman's arms straightaway. It was Ben, covered by some rough sacking that had previously contained building material. The boy's face was pale and dirty. He gazed around uncertainly and was gasping for breath. Around his mouth could be seen the remains of some leaves and grass.

"Water, quickly water!" shouted the policeman. Before Tony could touch his son, one of the workers offered him water. Ben drank with enthusiasm, and his face already began to look better and more alive. Only then could his father cuddle his lost child.

Later at home, when Ben was held and being comforted in his mum's arms, the family learned about the mystery of his disappearance. Andy had been collected by his father earlier than arranged, which had left Ben on his own. Ben had remembered that Andy's home was somewhere on the edge of Sandgate and had decided to go and explore where it was, but when he ventured into the shrubby area, he was lost. Disorientated and tired, he took a rest and fell asleep. Over the days that followed, he didn't meet anybody to ask where he was and was worried that if he did, they would call the police and he might get in trouble. Hungry and weak, he found shelter under a shrub or in a cave. It was the policeman and his dog who had eventually saved his life, in the middle of Sandgate's woody area.

For a long time afterwards, a ghostly rumour circulated about a lost child whose unhappy wailing could be heard near the Zig Zag path and caves at night.

14

Hilary and Nigel (R.I.P.)

by Paul W Robinson

Hilary sighed as she looked around her new home. At the age of fifty-five she was alone for the first time. Ever. She had lived with her parents until she married Nigel, thirty-five years before. She sighed again, and, this time, added a shake of her head. Nigel had begun to develop health issues, many of which seemed to begin with "a': angina, asthma, ankylosing spondylitis... He was becoming increasingly less mobile. He refused to give up his pipe and as a result his emphysema had been getting worse, too. He had, finally and reluctantly, been persuaded to move from the "smoke' to the seaside for his health. Just after contracts were exchanged, Nigel visited his London studio for what would turn out to be the last time. On the way home he crashed his car and died

The new house, in Folkestone, was beautiful. They could not have afforded anything like this in London. It was part of a brand-new estate - built on a brownfield site on Park Farm Road, a road leading to and from the M20. The estate of brand-new houses had previously been a school; it was known as the school estate. The house was a lot more spacious than Hilary was used to. It had three bedrooms, two bathrooms and three toilets in total, and a lovely big kitchen. All this space, for a woman now alone.

It was the kitchen, that had sold the house to her. What a change from the little galley kitchen in their old flat. So much storage space...and drawers. In their previous home there had been a small number of cupboards, but no drawers. It would seem a small thing to anyone else, but now she could store and retrieve utensils she wanted without bending her back or craning her neck. For his part, Nigel had "bagsed' the front bedroom for his studio, because of the light.

For years she had begged Nigel to move away somewhere - somewhere they could afford a nice house, but oh no. He "needed to be in London for his work." Although, there hadn't been much work done in the last year or two! And they had lived in their cramped flat, unable to entertain because they simply didn't have the space. She could only have her friends round one at a time.

She looked around. A third sigh. All those boxes to empty - with no-one to help! With two it was almost fun, emptying boxes; fun, finding things unexpectedly; fun, deciding where the items should go. Now it was simply a chore.

"*Oh well, better get started,*' she thought. She set about unpacking enough boxes so that she could settle herself in, with at least a minimum level of comfort. She chose the large back bedroom with its en suite shower room as her main. The bedroom at the front would be the guest room. All the things that were not immediately to be used were piled in there. It was packed solid with boxes - containing, amongst other things, Nigel's painting supplies and his clothes. In here, in what should have been his studio, she could smell him so strongly. It was an odd mixture of oil paint, his Dunhill pipe tobacco, and Old Spice – his favourite aftershave. It was old fashioned, but he loved it. It had become harder and harder to get hold of, but he would not be weaned from it, no matter how she tried to tempt him with nicer, more modern scents. It offended her sensitive nose. The stink of it clung to his clothes and art materials, and other possessions like limpet to a rock.

One by one and day by day the number of boxes decreased. In a few short weeks, the unpacking was more or less done. Hilary stood up one day from the last emptied box and stretched the kinks out of her back. She surveyed her domain with pride. The new house was looking good. It had been extremely hard work. She had given Nigel's clothes to charity- to the British Heart Foundation. They had been so helpful to her after her heart attack years before. The "myocardial infarction' had been a wake-up call for her. She lost her excess weight and got herself fit; she had had no symptoms now for years. So, it was the BHF that reaped the meagre harvest of her bereavement.

She donated Nigel's art materials to a local special school, the Beacon. The school's head of art collected the materials from her. There was the professional artist's easel, there was canvas, there were papers of various kinds, ditto paints, brushes, pastels, charcoal sticks...all of the highest quality. The teacher was thrilled to bits. Hilary received a nice card from the children at the school, thanking her for the lovely gifts. The card touched her; it made her smile.

In the front bedroom, the myriad boxes had been replaced by a farmhouse-style double bed, bedside cabinets, and a wardrobe – for the clothes of any friends, who might come to stay for a little break by the sea. Hilary had put the furniture up herself, from flat packs. It hadn't been as hard as Nigel always made it seem! She gave a nod of satisfaction as she closed the door. It was odd, but in spite of getting rid of all Nigel's things and airing the room thoroughly, she could still smell that particular blend of tobacco and Old Spice. She shrugged. The smell would go away eventually.

She had put all of Nigel's paintings in the loft. It was too painful to look at them at the moment, especially the nudes – he seemed to have an endless supply of beautiful young models. Those paintings, she would sell – once the news of his death had pushed up the prices sufficiently. In the meantime, she had never had so much money. His life insurance policies had been very generous, especially given his health problems. Later perhaps, she thought she might hang some of his nicer paintings around the house. He had done some lovely landscapes, including some delightful views of the forest.

Their London base was in Walthamstow. Epping Forest was on their doorstep. As part of her rehabilitation, after her heart attack, she had gone for long walks under the trees exploring the little paths away from the main bridle paths, enjoying nature. Often while walking she would see deer – both muntjac and fallow deer - and a whole range of birds. In the early summer they sang fit to burst. Occasionally, as she walked across a glade or plain, a green woodpecker would fly up from the ground with its distinctive "yaffle'. It would be nice to have his watercolours as a reminder of those walks. No doubt there would be new walks to explore, here in Folkestone. There would be the seashore, of course, and from her bedroom upstairs she could see the hills outside the town. They called to her. According to Google, a Roman camp had been on top of one of those hills. You could even see France - on a clear day.

At first there was so much to do that she had felt overwhelmed. Paperwork had never been her forte, Nigel handled business matters. She had had to arrange the funeral, sort out the finances: - including the will and the two life insurance policies, and then there was the fallout from the house move. She spoke to him frequently, as the bereaved often will.

"I gave you a good send-off, you would have been pleased. Lots of people came. I met some of your models. They seemed, nice - most of them. I was rather proud of the way I arranged everything. Not such a nincompoop as you thought!" she said to him early one morning, as she dusted the front bedroom. "And while we're on that subject, I always knew about your women, you know. I could always tell. Did you think that Old Spice would cover up Chanel, or Burberry? There was one who wore Britney Spears's "Curious." I'm guessing she was very young? One of your student models probably. No wonder you wanted your studio well away from the flat!

I used to go around perfume shops, to identify the different perfumes. There was one you kept returning to, the one that wears Chanel. Is that the one you were planning to leave me for?"

There was a sudden waft of tobacco. What on earth had she disturbed in her dusting? She left the room, coughing, and shut the door.

The call of the hills could not be denied. Later that morning, she essayed her first walk. She pushed on all the way to the Roman camp. It was two and a half miles away, not too far, but uphill all the way - a steep climb. It had been a stiff five miles by the time she got home, and she was exhausted. It brought on an attack of angina, the first for some time. Nonetheless, she felt good, she had enjoyed it. She took her nitro-glycerine spray and gradually felt better. She ran herself a luxurious bath in her lovely spacious new bathroom.

Later, just for fun she had a look at a dating website. It was called "mature and single." Why not? After all, she was both now.

It was some weeks later that she plucked up her courage and went on some dates. Just a coffee in the Eleto Chocolate Café, in town - or a drink at a local pub, like the Black Bull, accessible through a pedestrian alleyway she found. Among some so-so experiences and at least one disastrous one, there were one or two men who seemed really quite nice. She thought that, given time, she might take things to a more physical level with them. Her sex life with Nigel had not been great. She had come to resent that he was having a nice time with his young models, poor things, while she was putting up with his noisy, rough, and rather perfunctory attentions at home.

It was the first time in her life that she had gone on dates. She recalled how strict her Roman Catholic parents had been. She came from a tiny village. Marriageable men were very few and far between. Her parents would have liked her to meet a "nice' boy at church, then courting and a long engagement, followed by a big wedding.

By contrast she met Nigel. It was when she went to try a beginners' painting session. Nigel was the teacher, tall, bearded, urbane, and handsome. He was approaching forty and recently divorced, the sympathy she felt for him turned to warmer feelings. He told her she was beautiful; no-one had ever done that; and that he would like to paint her, nude – scandalous, but thrilling at the same time!

He swept her off her feet. After class one day, she lost her virginity in the back of his Bedford van. He seemed so glamorous, so urbane; he told her how talented he was, and she swallowed it whole.

Much to the chagrin of her parents they were married in a bare two months, in a register office. It was only after they married and began to move in artistic circles, she found out that Nigel was not well-regarded by fellow artists. At the time she believed that marriage was about getting behind your husband and supporting him. She pushed from behind. She arranged exhibitions, built up his publicity. Gradually he became more successful.

She persuaded him to explore new forms – it was her idea for him to increase his life drawing, to produce more nudes – nudes sold...

"I shot myself in the foot there, didn't I?" she said to Nigel one day, as she was getting ready for another date. "Well, I got my revenge in the end. It's amazing what you can find on the internet these days...including how to tamper with a car so that no-one will find out. I wasn't going to be stuck with becoming your carer, pushing you round the hills of Folkestone in a wheelchair, no thank you! Now I'm going to enjoy myself. I have a date this evening with Tom. Lovely name. Tomcat Tom. He's very nice, much nicer than you. He's younger than I am, and very handsome. He's a widower, like me. I'm going to bring him back here and see what happens."

She finished her make-up and dressed with care. She had on her new sexy underwear – something else she had got from the internet. She admired her trim figure in the mirror. She looked years younger than her age. Yes, tonight was the night. She had been on four dates with Tom. It was time to move it to the "next level..."

The next morning a distraught Tom was speaking to a motherly and sympathetic woman police sergeant.

"I don't really know what happened. We spent the evening making love, she seemed to enjoy it...After a bit we both went to sleep, then I woke up in the night, and she was clutching her chest. She grabbed that spray thing and sprayed it into her mouth, then her face changed, she looked like she had seen..."

"A ghost?"

"No," he said thoughtfully, "more like she had seen her own death, coming for her. It was horrible. She sat up, and fought for breath, she said "Nigel." It was really clear. Then she collapsed."

The police officer took the indicated spray and examined it. "Nitro-glycerine spray" she read. "To be taken as required." She sniffed it, and a frown creased her face. "Smell that." She said, "some sort of perfume."

Tom took the spray and sniffed it. "I remember this," he said. "My father used it. It's Old Spice!"

15

Up on the Ground

by Chani Barnes

Nothing is lucid, my surroundings but a blotch in my sight.

An ever-lasting throb and numb feeling through my frail figure.

A migraine flushing around my system, destroying any presence of sensation.

My toes are as if they have never noticed the floor. Like how a pappus floats forever in the wind, seeking a field to rest.

I pinpoint myself at the old pictures. I stand here before the snack bar disconnected, far from my frame.

I have limited recognition of those around me.

Scanning my whereabouts, I seek out my fellow companions. Peace and pleasure running all over their faces.

They stole right by me, but no greeting was exchanged. As if I was no one,

no one they knew.

Confusion sticks me down to the ground, which I have no feeling of.

Is it my attire? Does it seem unrecognisable?

Or my hair, that hasn't been changed in a lifetime?

I bellow out "Anyone? Can you see me?" But nothing...

Not a peep...

I am to be unheard, viewed yet unseen.

I hurry to what I thought was my loyal kin, but nothing arises.

I am still a drifting body, whom no one recognises.

I want answers. I want knowledge of this odd situation.

Puzzlement fills me like a fragile glass.

I find myself adjacent to a towering man.

As my words diffuse out of my lips, this chap reaches out, grasping his drink.

I should have felt a thud

But no, just a cold spear piercing my cage.

The notion occurs: I'm simply a vibrating echo.

Here as a thought, memory almost.

16

Do You Believe in Ghosts?

by Karen Marwood

BACKGROUND

This is a true account from 2019.

Have you ever seen a ghost, and do you believe in them or are they wild figments of our imagination? Sometimes we hear about all sorts of spiritual happenings, but my view has always been that I will believe it when I see it. People can give such accurate descriptions with so much passion that it is hard not to think that they have seen something. This is about my experience and I will leave you to make up your own minds!

Last year I organised an event for my writing group "Write by The Sea." It was held in The Chambers bar, an excellent venue for this all-day event as the surroundings, small areas, separated by alcoves, enabled the authors to have their own space. Over twenty authors attended, and I have to say it went off without a hitch. On the other hand, I was very stressed as it was the first time I had arranged anything like this. I knew that my mind was full of authors, books, space, hosts, food, advertising and the one thing I couldn't control, how many people would come? So yes, my mind was full of everything book-related, not that I realised that at the time, as you don't, you just get on with everything.

I organise events every month for my writing group, so we invite someone along each month to do with books; could be an author, illustrator, photographer or others involved in the process of making a book and selling it. We also had a door at the "Living Advent Calendar" event at The Chambers which involved us writing stories then reading them and acting them out to the public in a very short time allowance. One of the events planned for the following year was to have been "An evening with Shakespeare" so I'd been keeping a look out for things I could use for this event.

THE PLACE

I live in Folkestone on my own in a ground floor flat with garden, where I have lived for over twelve years. This particular evening, my friend was staying on the sofa bed in the lounge room. I have never experienced anything like what I am about to tell you. As you can realise from the background, I did have an awful lot going on in my life so yes, my mind was active and overfull, did that have anything to do with what happened? I don't know but you can decide.

THE OCCURRENCE

I woke in the middle of the night; the room wasn't pitch black so I could see. I was lying on the right side of my double bed where there is a gap of about two metres before the bedroom door. As I looked up, I saw someone standing there, slightly bending over looking down at me! You would expect to be scared and trying to run from the bed and the room, but I kept blinking my eyes to try to make whatever it was go away. He didn't. It was a male from years ago; he had one of those ruff collars standing up round his neck and he was wearing a hat. I told him to go away, which he ignored so I said to him that I would turn the light on and that would make him go. Do ghosts go in light? I have no idea but this one did. I then turned the light off and went back to sleep, which is again strange as normally I would be awake and then reading to be able to go back to sleep.

The next morning, over a cup of tea, I told my friend all about it, and we tried to work out who it was that I had seen. It was in the olden days as you could tell by his clothes; it was an older man. We thought about writing and books and came up with a few names, but nothing really felt right to me until we said Shakespeare! I then looked up a picture of him and then went very cold as yes, it was him all right. So, why was Shakespeare visiting me?

The following week I saw him once again but this time he was lying along the top of my wardrobe looking down at me. All very strange and not at all frightening.

On another occasion when again I had a friend staying, I had another visitor who turned out to be Shakespeare's wife, Anne Hathaway! I tried turning over and ignoring her, but she too stayed until I put the light on. I could describe her exactly as her picture, although I had never seen a picture of her until then, not that I could remember. None of the apparitions spoke, thank goodness; I think that would have sent me running. Was I so calm because I was half asleep?

The final visit took a while to piece together but after long discussions with my friend and looking at photos I realised that my visitor was Shakespeare's daughter! This was really shocking and confusing; I did not understand what was going on and wanted some answers. I even spoke to a medium, but no one knew why this was happening or could even throw any light at all on the matter. Do any ghosts talk?

Now, why were they all visiting me, what did Shakespeare and his family want from me?

To this day, I do not know why, and I have never seen any of them again or indeed anyone else, which I felt a bit sad about as it was all so amazing. Was it just my mind and eyes making me see things, can that actually happen? It did seem very real to me but why wasn't I scared? It is all a mystery that I will leave here for you to make up your own minds about.

Is there any truth in ghosts?

17

Invisible Obstacle

by Jana Chatters

With our senior years approaching, we faced a decision to exchange our home in Essex for another in a calmer, green area. A few picturesque areas and places we had adored on our holidays and trips ran through our heads, but suddenly stopped!

Our sight was on the South-East part of the British Isles, in the county of Kent with marsh land, fishing villages, beaches, the Isle of Thanet and woodland.

"This is my cup of tea, Keith!" My sentence sounded enthusiastic and real.

I meant, we could find there everything that we liked. Rolling countryside, woodland, castles and châteaux, sea coast with beaches, in easy striking distance of France for short trips or longer holidays.

These facts prompted us to organise a search to make sure our imagination was not distorted and to find out more about the area.

"I think a few nights at a hotel or B&B, would be enough? To walk around, find out what the local facilities are like. Are you up for that?" asked Keith. My answer was a simple nod, smiling happily, full of enthusiasm to set off as soon as possible. Having decided to start in the Folkestone area, an internet search threw up quite a few possibilities for accommodation.

"Look at this! A perfect example of a fairy tale building!" Straight away, we adored the classical Edwardian-style Grand Hotel. A majestic building, a popular holiday destination for royalty in Edwardian times, with its rooms and dining areas sparkling with light, surrounded by green and with a sea view too. Once Keith had booked our trip to "Paradise," we shared our plans with our neighbour Josh.

"Are you really planning to stay at the Grand in Folkestone? That's a nightmare!" he replied, his eyes widening. "That's a Haunted Hotel! I am positive. I've heard it from a number of their guests and independently of each other too!"

Within a few minutes, we had learnt of dull humming noises, a human shadow circling around guests' rooms, or a 'night cleaner' who disturbed the night silence; others too.

After Josh left, we were lost for words, but only for a few moments. We don't like gossip or being mystified by somebody who has never actually been to the place. Our decision was too strong. It couldn't just be cancelled by some beer lover.

When we arrived for the start of our holiday on Folkestone's Leas, we were amazed!

On this pleasant, sunny September day, the sea looked as if it had been painted turquoise blue, hemmed with a gold coast, contrasting with the nature around. When our eyes caught the Grand with its Union Jack on top of the Dome, we knew we were in the right place. After several minutes, we opened the door of our twin room. Our joy was endless. Light, airy, with a sea view and balcony! At that moment, we forgot about the cost and our budget and just enjoyed it!

After a delicious dinner and a short walk, we adored the unspoilt views from our room on the second floor.

"Well done!" My husband was full of praise. After talking over our plans for the next day, we felt tired and went to bed earlier than we normally did.

Some cold air blowing on my face woke me up. I sat up on the bed. It was still dark, but I could see the balcony door was fully open. I could have sworn Keith had closed it. Slipping from the bed to close it, I could see somebody sitting there! Maybe a man, his long legs stretched out? Frightened to death, I started screaming and woke Keith. I was speechless, standing like a statue, but managed to move my arm in the direction of the balcony. Keith immediately caught on that something had happened. He looked in the direction I showed but told me all he could see were two chairs and a small table. He mentioned that he could feel a light breeze and hear the humming sea but that was all.

He didn't seem convinced about my explanation of what had happened. But when he saw me next morning, pale, still scared, and after listening to my story, he decided to change our accommodation. During our discussion at the Reception desk about our reason for leaving, we must have looked slightly ridiculous. The receptionist turned his head in a negative gesture but kept smiling. He gave me a pitying look and apologised for our unpleasant night.

With no further comment from my husband, we walked along the Leas towards the town centre. But after a few metres, Keith stopped at a bench and asked me to sit down and take some fresh air. I happily agreed to calm down and enjoy the view. Keith took out of his briefcase a sheet of paper with a list of other hotels and B&Bs.

"Here you are!" I could hear his happy call after a couple of minutes. He pointed towards a large light building just a few metres across the green. I couldn't see any sign or name.

"This is the Clifton Hotel – Best Western. It was the first hotel we chose! But the Grand looked more attractive and ancient, do you remember?" I agreed - still feeling guilty about our problem.

"Good morning. Welcome to the Clifton Hotel!" After we had talked over what we wanted, the receptionist suggested we wait for a cup of coffee or go for a short walk, while our room was being prepared. Or we could have immediately a more expensive apartment. The next room he offered was the same price as The Grand and we were enjoying our room within minutes - on the top floor, overlooking the garden behind the hotel, quiet, a big bathroom, a fireplace, a sitting area suitable for a VIP!

"What a relief!" Keith announced silently, spreading out into a big old-fashioned chair. I started to tidy up my belongings, feeling happy about our decision.

Just before lunch time we started exploring the town centre, and carried on down the Old High Street, to the Harbour. Even if it was redolent of fish, we adored that little spot, so full of character. We ordered a sea food lunch at a street stall and took our places at the nearest wooden table and bench, directly overlooking the fishing harbour.

"At the genuine spot it tastes better, doesn't it?" We could hear, behind our backs, the voices of a lady and a gentleman.

"You are right!" we answered, smiling our thanks.

"Are you local, or here by chance?" the man continued.

"Just for a short stay to do some exploring for a new place for our retirement." Keith replied.

"We might even have decided already!" I added.

"Not a bad choice. We like this area too. We're from Maidstone. It's not far away, but we come here for a break, quite often!" The lady agreed with us.

"And we always stay at the Hotel Burstin." The man pointed his finger in the direction of a giant building, shaped like a cruise ship. "And you?"

"At the Clifton Hotel on The Leas. It is more expensive, but once a year...!" The man frowned slightly, and I noticed Keith was a little embarrassed. But the man continued:

"We've heard very different comments from other guests of the Clifton. Haven't we?" His wife nodded.

Our conversation with the couple turned to more pleasant topics. They told us about a few other local attractions, and, after a further short chat, we shook hands and said our goodbyes.

Later that afternoon as the sun began to set, we really appreciated our new accommodation. Through the wide-open door to the balcony, we were able to enjoy the Green at the back of the hotel, listen to the birds singing and sip the afternoon tea the waiter had delivered to our room. We were both tired, but Keith seemed more exhausted than me! Unwillingly, I took a short shower. As I walked from the bathroom towards the bed, I could already hear he was in a deep sleep.

I went to sleep too but shortly after, something interrupted me. I was in a deep sleep but the dream that woke me up was extremely frightening. This wasn't a dream now. I was awake, in pitch blackness, feeling very uneasy. Somebody was standing just beside my bed or was it a silhouette or shadow? Fairly tall, moving slightly... I was terrified, lost control. My body was shaking, but in several seconds the vision had vanished. Our room was back to normal again. I could only hear my husband murmuring slightly at being disturbed. It was one hour after midnight. When I finally managed to get off to sleep, I could hear the first bird song of the morning.

"Morning! Did you sleep well?" Keith was looking at me, happily. I was quiet, not my usual chatty self as I got dressed.

"You look rather pale?" he inquired.

"Thank you, it was OK, but I had rather a disturbed night," I answered and continued with my morning routine, intending not to mention anything to him.

Trying to make conversation, we went to the restaurant for breakfast. As we passed Reception, we were greeted by a new receptionist we hadn't seen yesterday.

"Are you the new guests? Did you have a quiet night?"

His greetings were as effusive as a waterfall, and he looked so happy.

"Thank you, couldn't have been better. My wife had a bit of an unsettled night, but we only got here yesterday, and she was tired."

We were about to continue on our way when the clerk interrupted us.

"Just a second! What's the number of your room?"

"No 111 on the first floor!" said Keith, obviously bored now and wanting to move on. But he noticed the clerk's happy face had vanished. He was a still as a stone and answered in a whisper: "Thank you Sir!"

After a few seconds, as we entered the restaurant, we could hear him again speaking more loudly this time.

"I'll check that out, Sir, and let you know!"

Our buffet breakfast from a luxurious menu, with a chance to enjoy the garden view, distracted us from any thoughts of nocturnal disturbances.

"What about today? Shall we go for a walk in the country?" Keith waved a brochure of the Folkestone area which told us that just a short distance from the town centre we could find an amazing view point, with views all around the area and the coast. I was happy with that idea and in a few minutes, we parked under Castle Hill.

The dominant hill of the North Downs impressed me straight away. After a short climb, we had a bird's eye view of Folkestone and were taking deep breaths of the fresh sea air. This natural video refreshed us enough to extend our walk for another hour.

After our walk down the hill, we were ready for a break and, attracted by the old part of town, we found a coffee room in the Old High Street. Because it was crowded, we happily shared a table with two youngsters. They were students at the local University and liked the charming old classic area very much. Chatty, cheerful, full of energy, they impressed us.

"Wow! Are you guests at the Clifton Hotel?" was the reaction of one of the boys, when we explained what had brought us to the area. We both nodded, and we chatted about the nice position and the tradition. Yet again, there was a mention of it being haunted.

Luckily, we had nice refreshments, we were enjoying our walk and were generally in a good mood. So, we both gave them a smile, thanked them for their company and off we went.

Browsing through the brochures and leaflets we had picked up during our stay, we were resting after dinner in the hotel lounge.

"Excuse me Sir!" We could hear the voice of the Receptionist behind us.

"After hearing of your disturbed sleep, I found out that there'd been a noise underneath your room. There is a utility room down there for meetings and such like and the hotel staff use it to store furniture. They started rather early this morning. Very sorry for the inconvenience! The Hotel Manager would like to offer you a complimentary snack and a glass of fizz each!"

Wide smile again, face shining.

Astounded, with big thanks, we were served with - and enjoyed – an almost royal snack.

"Keith, I feel guilty!" I whispered, but my husband, influenced by the sparkling wine, laughed and continued our drinks.

"What disturbed and frightened me was just after midnight! Do you understand? We are actually cheating, we shouldn't be having this!"

"Come on, dear!" My husband was in a very relaxed mood. Putting his arm round my shoulders, he led the way to our room.

Tonight, we missed watching the birds and didn't linger over the view of the hotel gardens. Keith's bedtime routine was much shorter than normal, and I felt unusually tired and forgot about what had happened over the last few days. But there was something disturbing all the same. Our bed seemed a little shaky, or Keith moved, I can't describe it.

To my big surprise, when I woke up, Keith was gone! I sat up, looked around and I could hear water running. I was relieved when he came out of the shower, but instead of his typical smile, he looked at me with a sleepy, blank face.

Before I could ask, he started to complain: "Nightmare! I was disturbed, hell! I thought it was you, somebody standing there, then they vanished!" He pointed towards the balcony. "But you were sleeping calmly!" I listened to him and nodded.

"You see, I wouldn't have wished that on you, but perhaps now you can understand me!"

"Good Morning Sir and Madam! I hope you had a calm night?" Our greetings came from the other receptionist, with a sweet smile, who wished us a good breakfast and a happy day.

We both nodded our thanks and continued towards the restaurant. I can't remember us ever having taken a meal together in silence. That morning we did, but I interrupted the silence in the end.

"What's the plan for today, darling?" Keith looked towards the window. The bright sun and the blue sky had changed his mood.

"I would like to get up somewhere high," I continued. "I need to breathe and wake up."

The right place, according to my husband, was on top of the cliffs at the village of Capel-le-Ferne. A view down to the sea of the English Channel has special power and magic. Our refuge became the Coffee Room on the cliff, and, after a little longer, absorbing that amazing atmosphere and sipping our coffee, our minds were made up. We bought a property in Folkestone!

Author's Notes

The Grand and The Clifton are both haunted, according to local legend. Room 111 at the Clifton is where a lady, given the name Jane Doe because her real name wasn't known, is said to have committed suicide after a fight with her lover. Her ghost is described as wearing a nightgown, and evoking feelings of great sadness and misery.

18
Where Old Ghosts Meet
by
Tony Quarrington

A biting breeze and thin drizzle denote December's inevitable but uninvited return. Twilight descends on the ancient churchyard.

Never has the phrase "quiet as the grave" seemed more apt.

As I pause to tie my bootlaces by the Town Cross, venue for the making of mayors for many centuries, my body shudders as a young woman brushes past me, the hem of her blue dress grazing the grass border, and her white headpiece fluttering in the wind. She carries provisions for the poor - bread, leeks and a small flagon of beer - in a round wicker basket, forswearing another potentially lucrative tryst with a Northumbrian nobleman, orchestrated by her frustrated father.

Her head bowed, she whispers *"Good evening, sir, God be with you."* Before I can frame an intelligible response, she disappears behind the west window.

Composing myself as best I can in the circumstances, I shamble on past the crumbling tombs, narrowly avoiding a collision with a rat, scurrying across my path to the sanctuary of the lopsided lychgate leading into Church Street. The *Pullman* pub is empty, save for a few flickering candles and a lone member of bar staff deep in conversation with his mobile phone.

The lanterns of Rendezvous Street are unusually dim, and the restaurants are sparsely populated.

The stillness is unnerving, but strangely thrilling.

I turn into the narrow, twisting, rain drenched street that slides down towards the harbour.

Many months have elapsed since chaotic, cacophonous *Charivari* had snaked up that old thoroughfare, all drums and whistles and cymbals, and other less conventional instruments. More recently, the ground had groaned beneath the burden of polished, red-laced *Doc Martens*, worn by follicly challenged pilgrims lumbering towards *Gillespie's* and *The Ship* for an afternoon of *Special Brew,* and worship at the altars of *Prince Buster* and *The Specials*.

I am alone.

But am I?

The fog in my brain mirrors the slowly enveloping mist approaching from the bottom of the hill. Images of times past in this salty, saintly town start to consume my thoughts.

Nothing is quite what it seems.

My longing for one last lingering look at the dazzling, daily alchemy conjured up in the rock shop near the top of the street Dickens christened a "crippled ladder" is soon answered. The heady, fashionable aromas of craft beer and Nicaraguan coffee cannot compete with the memory of the sickly-sweet perfume radiating from that beloved spot, where, nose squashed against the glass, a small boy gasped in awe at the thick, long sticks of heaven being rolled.

"Let me in at the front, Michael, you've been stood there for ages," pleads his tearful younger sister, Anna, her view obscured by the taller girl stood in front of her.

"Have they started giving out the bags of broken bits yet?" another boy bellows from further back in the crowd.

A sudden, excited scrum confirms his suspicion as I catch an intoxicating whiff of granulated sugar.

It was often claimed that if *Rowlands* were to shut its doors for good, Folkestone would die; a prediction, thankfully, since proven dramatically wrong,

I stumble into *Steep Street Coffee House* for cake and cappuccino, a combination that never fails to comfort. I am their last customer of the day and the staff, without being obtrusive, are cleaning up around me. The self-styled *Folkestone Poet h*as vacated his customary sales pitch across the cobbles at *Big Boys Burger,* his heavy overcoat and leather balaclava no longer a match for the diminishing temperatures.

I pass by *Marley's* - or what I thought was *Marley's.* From a dark upstairs room, redolent of patchouli and cigarette smoke, a loud, piercing jukebox exhorts me to *"go to San Francisco"* - a seductive reminder of the original *Summer of Love* on such a bleak winter's evening.

Two young men in afghan coats, and a messy profusion of facial hair, are huddled at the foot of the crippling, crumbling Bayle Steps.

"Hey man, how's it going?"

"Far out, whatcha doing' tonight?"

"Going' to Archies. The Lonely Ones are playing".

Nice. I hear there's some hot Swedish chicks in town too".

"That's settled then, Archie's it is".

"Yeah, and I could kill for one of his salami rolls right now".

I start to follow them through the door, only to find that the closer I get, the scene dissolves in the moist air, and I am left once more outside *Marley's* rather than the *Acropolis*.

The piercing cold slices through my flimsy denim jacket and hastens my progress to the bottom of the street. Everything is still again as I try to rationalise the scenes I have encountered in the past half hour.

I cross a deserted Tram Road car park and pass under the arch by *Ovenden's* old forge into the empty fish market, tiptoeing around the grimy puddles that tend to settle there, whether it has rained or not.

A solitary gull plods apologetically past, pining for Spring and the reopening of *Chummy's* and *Bob's* seafood stalls, when it will again be afforded means, motive and opportunity to ambush tourists for their fish and chips and tubs of whelks.

Pausing outside *The Shell Shop*, I appear to have stepped into an earlier time again. Men in cloth caps and heavy, seaweed encrusted boots trudge up the slipway opposite, lobster pots and herring nets half empty after an exhausting and disheartening shift. They slap their meagre catch on the floor of *Fish Shed One,* light cigarettes and congregate in whispered conversation.

'Darkie" Fagg, "Cottage" Featherbe and "Lobby" Spearpoint are leaning on the railing and reminiscing about better days, while Old Ned Saunders, retired these ten years, is mending the sprat nets for a "free" pint or two in The *Oddfellows Arms* later this evening.

On the Stade, wives and daughters juggle the demanding tasks of cleaning fish and supervising the smaller, and not so clean, children.

Observing this picture, it is difficult to gauge which gender had the tougher life.

Meanwhile, grubby, barefoot young boys, oblivious to the dedication and drudgery of their elders all around them, chalk stumps on the wall of *Clouts Alley*.

"I'll be Jack "Obbs, you can be Clarrie Grimmett. I'll 'it you into the "arbour, every time, just you see" brags nine-year old Harry Sharp.

But with his first delivery, Clarrie, better known about these parts as Edmund, and, in later years, "La La" Taylor, traps Jack in front of his wicket and appeals for leg before.

"Owzat! Got you with me flipper, pom."

A heated dispute follows, culminating in the great English batsman hurling his bat against the wall and storming off in the direction of Redman's boat builders.

His mother, ankle deep in half-gutted dogfish and three scruffy toddlers, calls:

"Harry, your tea is ready. And find your brother before you come in".

"Five more minutes, mum. I've got to bowl Don Bradman out first. it won't take long".

"Five more minutes, my arse - you've got thirty seconds. This tea won't wait. If you don't get to the table soon, the other kids will have your share".

A case of bad mum stopped play.

As this scene of family harmony evaporates, I hear, from across the harbour, a sergeant major's ear-splitting admonition to *"Step Short,"* to a long procession of uniformed men stomping down the slope from the Leas above.

The rhythmic sound of boots on concrete is accompanied by raucous renditions of *Pack up Your Troubles in Your Old Kit Bag* and *It's a Long Way to Tipperary,* as the soldiers march to the waiting ships that will take them to the Western Front.

But there is one last treat before their sombre adventure begins.

Inside the harbour station waiting room, two formidable middle-aged women adjust their pinafores and rearrange any curls that have slipped beneath their flower bestrewn boaters. They inspect the massive urns containing the last hot, strong tea most of these men will ever drink.

"Come on boys, form a straight line, you don't have long, you know," Flora Jeffrey cries out with a tinge of regret in her voice, while her sister Margaret cuts thin slices of trench cake and bread pudding to complete what, for many of these condemned men, will be their last meal.

"And don't forget to sign the visitors' book before you do".

"All right, all right, you sound like me muvver - nag, nag, nag", one private who claims to be twenty- one but looks barely sixteen, retorts, as he lurches towards Margaret and slurs:

"Give us a kiss".

But before he can perfect this unwise manoeuvre, a grizzled veteran of Mafeking and Ladysmith yanks him back by his collar and barks:

"Show the ladies some respect, young 'un'. You ain't in the playground now, y'know."

"Sorry, old timer, I didn't mean nuffin' by it, it was just a bit of fun".

Flora chuckles: *"You got off lightly there, my boy, that's nothing to what Margaret would have done to you if you'd got any nearer!".*

An outpouring of communal hilarity is unleashed, and the embarrassed teenager slinks back into the anonymity of the crowd.

I separate from the excited, but fearful, throng with the final strains of *Keep the Home Fires Burning* ringing in my ears and join the boardwalk that connects the station with the base of the thirty-year-old water lift along the beach to the west.

But I have hardly stepped foot on the old railway sleepers before finding myself in the midst of a large conglomeration of buildings, including a swimming pool, boating lake and fairground rides.

As I try to take all this in, a crew cut kid in knitted cardigan and khaki shorts can be seen rushing into a huge, dimpled dome that is destined to be his whole world for the next two weeks. He will never tire of rolling a penny for plastic motor cars or shooting a steel ball into a hole for packets of mints.

His father and mother, the latter clutching a wad of what appear to be tickets, frown as they dismount from the blue plastic seats they have occupied for the past two hours, where they had been subjected to an increasingly annoying loop of "legs eleven", "two little ducks, twenty two" and "two fat ladies' eighty eight".

The boy drags himself from the penny pusher slot machine and scampers towards them in a frenzy of excitement.

"How many wins did you get, mum?".

"Eight."

His heart sinks. *"Oh no, that big cuddly monkey on the bottom shelf is nine wins. Can you play some more games and win it for me?"*

"We don't have time, darling; besides dad and I want that nice set of tea trays that are eight wins. They will be just perfect for our TV dinners when we get home."

"Boring."

Feeling betrayed and despondent, the boy skulks off in the direction of the Runaway Coaster.

But he is soon appeased by a promise to go to his favourite fish and chip restaurant in Tontine Street for tea.

Intermittent drizzle and mist have given way to steady rain and a thickening gloom. Hungry and shivering, I resolve to return home.

Christmas lights bestride the street across the ragged rooftops, and retailers and restaurateurs contend for the accolade of best dressed window, though tonight there is nobody about to judge them.

Apart from the echo of my boots upon the sodden cobbles, silence is restored.

Until I reach *Archie's.*

From that same gloomy upstairs window from whence the Flowerpot Men had serenaded me two hours - and a hundred and fifty years - earlier, the Small Faces remind me that:

"It's all too beautiful".

After the battering my senses have taken this evening, I remain to be convinced of the veracity of this hypothesis.

So, I try, for the second time, to gain access to the old haunt of hippies and radicals.

As I take my first hesitant steps in its direction, fully expecting to find myself in *Marley's* again, the doors open of their own accord and I am permitted to enter.

And there, waiting to greet me, is the original owner, Mickey Argegrou, who is anxious to introduce me to his special guests for the night.

To my astonishment, Saint Eanswythe is here. The modest blue and white garments she had been wearing during our perfunctory encounter in the churchyard earlier have been replaced by a brightly coloured, patterned flowery dress and matching peaked hat. She is sampling her first ever cup of coffee and, judging by the uncharacteristic grimace that quickly follows, she is unlikely to order a second. Water from her own spring and the occasional small goblet of mead will remain her preferred tipples.

With the final troop ship of the day, *Engadine,* having set sail for Boulogne, and the *Mole Cafe* consequently closed, the indomitable Jeffrey sisters have swapped their pinafores for elegant three- quarter length dresses. They appear to be conducting a taste test of Mickey's famed rum babas, comparing them in the process with their revered fruit cake.

John Brickell, still in his overalls and safety cap, is here too. He has disappointed his vast army of young fans by holding back the remnants of today's rock rolling, handing the broken bits around to the grateful regulars, who find them a perfect accompaniment to their cocktails.

And Harry Sharp, grown in the past hour into a handsome young man, but still smarting from his first ball duck at the Clouts Alley Oval, is feeding the jukebox, while Old Ned Saunders, released from his net repairing duties, though not separated from his favourite fisherman's jumper, for the evening, is leading a communal sing along to the latest tune selected by Harry:

"Those were the days, my friend".

After the scenes I have witnessed this evening, I am inclined to agree.

19

N.K.G. (No Known Grave ... or...The Bells of St Eanswythe's)

by

Margaret Harland-Suddes

And performed by Mary Leadbetter and Margaret at the 2019 Folkestone Living Advent Calendar

Characters: The ghosts of a soldier represented by a Helmet. (S)

An airman represented by an Airman's Cap.(A)

Sound Effects: Machine guns, cannon fire, and warfare, loud but fading into the sound of the parish church bells, of St. Mary and St. Eanswythe's Church, Folkestone; they play loudly, then gradually fade and die.

Two ghostly figures appear within spotlights.

S... 187369 Corporal Smithers J...A German bomb blasted me into pieces in a shell hole on the Somme, in October 1916.

A... 236054 Pilot Officer Browne P...A Messerschmitt gunner blasted me out of the sky over Folkestone, in July 1940.

Together... All we ever wanted was for the fighting to stop. We wanted to live - and return home to a peaceful world.

S... I remember Folkestone. It was the last place in England I ever saw. It was March 1916 when they marched us down the cliff road to the ships waiting in the harbour, to begin our journey-of-no-return, to the battlefields in France. That was *The Great War;* it was meant to see the end of all wars. A week later I was slogging along up to my eyes in mud and bullets; then after six months of Hell, I was hung out on barbed-wire, and blown to bits on the Somme, by German guns.

A... We were young lads, eighteen years old and straight out of school, in September 1939. It seemed a glorious adventure to fly a Spitfire and fight for my country. No one ever said we were going to die. Your old war hadn't fixed anything, because in 1939 the Germans were at it again, trying to take over the world. That's how I ended up like this.

S... My family never knew where my scattered remains were. I wanted to be back home, here in England. I wanted to walk back up that cliff road and see the church again. They call it *The Road of Remembrance* now. I've kept wandering back here every year, hoping somebody would remember me, and I'd eventually find a place with my name and number on it, back here in Blighty.

A... It's true isn't it...All us restless ghosts are wandering about, searching for our own bit of hallowed ground; just a simple grave to call our own; something we've never been given!

S... Well you've heard the old saying, God answers all prayers in one of three ways... *Yes! No!... and, Not Yet!*

A... He hasn't answered any of my prayers yet so I must still be on His *Not Yet* list. Maybe there's still hope for me... but I doubt it.

S... So, what is it you're still praying for mate? You've been coming back here for a long time.

A... Pretty much the same as you, I guess. Just a piece of peaceful English soil with my name on it. Some sort of acknowledgement that I did my bit... just a place where I can rest easy, knowing I've finally made it home.

S... What actually happened to you, matey? Where did your bits get dumped?

A... Like I said, a Messerschmitt happened to me! I still remember Folkestone... We were based up there on the Downs, flying out of Hawkinge in June 1940. I saw the town every day from the cockpit of my Spitfire. We were kept busy all that summer fighting *The Battle of Britain.* They called this bit of England, *Hell-Fire Corner* in those days. This old church of St Eanswythe was a landmark for us, up here on the cliffs. Fine view they must've had of our dog-fights over the channel. But the bells were silent then--- never to be rung unless Hitler's invasion started. *Operation Sea Lion*, he called it... Mind you, it never did happen; our lads gave them a good seeing to, and that put paid to their invasion plans; we blew them out of these English skies. It was just bad luck that I bought it before the end of that September. That was when Goering changed his ruddy mind and started the Blitzkrieg on London instead. Evil so-and-so; he started bombing civilians, and the docks, to try and make Britain surrender.

S... I guess there were millions like us, mate. *Casualties of War...* We ended our days as just small parts of the wreckage called *Human History.* Just the unfortunate collateral damage...the cannon fodder...the victims needlessly sacrificed, because of the unfortunate blunders made by useless politicians. They say, those who refuse to learn from the terrible mistakes of the past, are destined to go on repeating them. I died in that Great War that was supposed to end all wars. Then, damn me, twenty-one years later they started another one. Damn all politicians; they make wars...but they rarely fight in them.

A... Well I'm fed up with lying forgotten in the mud beneath the English Channel. I want to have a proper place under the soil here in England...it's the least the powers-that-be could've done for me. Just give me a spot in a quiet corner of St Eanswythe's church-yard, and I'll rest content.

S... We're long forgotten mate... what we did doesn't matter anymore. Those damned politicians are all the same; they'll still be arguing and squabbling like spoilt kids another hundred years from now. They learn nothing... they care only about making themselves important... and lining their pockets.

A... Is there no one left who will speak for us? What guarantee is there that war is finished? Will they ever learn?

S... They make a bit of a fuss once a year, in November... On Armistice Day...but that's more to do with glory; a big show, with military bands, and parading about with medals and such. A load of posh people making speeches and laying wreathes...what do they really know about war?

Who really cares about remembering this was our land too?... We haven't forgotten...We died to defend their freedom; their future was guaranteed by our sacrifice... but they don't seem to learn anything from the lessons of History! You have to remember, mate... We're dead...Ghosts have no voice... There's no one left alive who speaks for us... We were just ordinary men...we never had a choice...we just took orders, we couldn't ask questions and had to accept how things were...DO and DIE... that was OUR job...No voice of our own at all...

Together... War is something no one ever really wins... The Christmas message tells us...Peace on Earth must prevail.

The bells begin to chime loudly again...fade out...END

20

The Signal-Man of Folkestone Harbour

by Mark Brophy

Arthur sat contentedly in an often too comfortable chair, reading. The fire hissed and popped as rainwater found its way down the chimney, but it was well alight with no fear of extinction. The howling wind, which had brought the rain in off the sea, rattled the thin window panes of the recently built box and whistled around the solid wooden door. A proud example of the new industrial age, the signal box stood on the viaduct next to the iron swing bridge, high above the harbour and shrouded by mist and spray. Below, boats banged together in the swell of the storm, though the harbour was calm compared to the maelstrom beyond the protective harbour walls. Every now and then the sea would slam against those walls with a crack like cannon fire.

Arthur was proud to be one of the first to man this box and treated it as he would his own home, regularly polishing the brass plates and chastising anyone that attempted to enter in dirty attire. "Cleanliness is next to Godliness" had been inscribed on the wall of his childhood home, a mantra he was determined to pass on to others!

On a normal winter's evening, he would have been busy. Train movements to and from the new harbour station had increased in recent weeks and the ebb and flow of ships from the continent was a sure sign that business was booming. But this night no wagons were being shunted in the yard, no squealing of wheels on worn tracks and there was no steady chuff of steam as the engines climbed the one in thirty gradient to Folkestone Junction. This night belonged to mother nature.

A few hours previously, the signalman had received a visitor.

"Stand there ya eejit and don't think you're coming in with those boots on!" shouted Arthur, only half as angry as he made out.

"Get out of my way ol' man and give me a drink."

Tommy, the young messenger boy, pushed past Arthur to pour some tea from the pot. Only Tommy could get away with talking to Arthur like that; he was cheeky but likeable. The son he'd never had. Arthur pushed the door shut against the wind as Tommy dripped towards the fire.

"So, is this a social call or do you actually have a message?" quizzed Arthur.

"There's a tree down across the junction, Mr O'Sullivan," said the lad, gulping down hot but nondescript tasting liquid. "Nothing's going to be moving for a while yet, it's that big oak, got struck by lightnin' - it's a mess up there, brought a signal down an' all."

"So, what you're telling me is that Folkestone Junction is blocked, and all trains are caped on all lines until the line is cleared. I do wish you'd learn to use correct terminology, Tommy, you'll need to if you're to become a proper railwayman." Arthur loved the language of his profession.

"S'pose," nodded Tommy with a wry smile. "Oh an' I brought you this. Thought you might get bored with no actual work to do stuck 'ere on this bridge in the wind," he laughed as he reached into his sodden coat to pull out a rather damp collection of papers.

"Household Words: A Flight by Charles Dickens," mouthed Arthur quietly as he read the cover page. Tommy fidgeted and scooped day-old dirt from his nails as Arthur fell silent, reading intently. He loved the written word and though he loved books never considered that anything he wrote would be good enough. No, writing should be reserved for those that can, he felt.

"Ha! Listen to this!" shouted Arthur excitedly as he quoted Mr. Dickens:

"I wonder why it is that when I shut my eyes in a tunnel I begin to feel as if I were going at an Express pace the other way. I am clearly going back to London, now. Compact Enchantress must have forgotten something and reversed the engine. No!

After long darkness, pale fitful streaks of light appear. I am still flying on for Folkestone. The streaks grow stronger—become continuous —become the ghost of day—become the living day—became I mean—the tunnel is miles and miles away, and here I fly through sunlight, all among the harvest and the Kentish hops."

"He must have written that after coming down here! Did I tell you I met him when he came to watch the Princess Clementine lay those submarine cables?"

"Only once or twice, Mr. O'Sullivan," said Tommy disinterestedly. "Well, thanks for the tea, I'm off now. Guvnor gave me the rest of the shift off as there won't be much else goin' on tonight." Tommy made for the door before Arthur could subject him to another rendition. Arthur waved him away without looking up, devouring this new text. After noting the evening's events in the register, he settled into the comfortable chair. He could have shut up shop for the night and returned home, nobody would have noticed, but the signal box was warm and less damp than his lodgings. Besides he had nothing to go home for and why use his own coal when the South Eastern Railway Company could provide it instead? Arthur locked the door and settled in for a cosy evening. The child of Irish immigrants, Arthur had determined from an early age that he would make something of himself. He had watched his father literally slogging his guts out as a navvy, digging canals and later laying railway lines. When his mother died giving birth to what would have been Arthur's sister, his father drowned the pain, and himself, in liquor. Determined that would not be his fate, Arthur keenly learned to read and write, opening his mind to opportunity. He loved fiction and Dickens in particular, who not only seemed to tell stories of lives he recognised, but also excited his imagination. Having met the man, he would read these stories not in his own voice, but in the voice of the author and at times became so consumed in the text as to forget his own identity entirely. This was the magic of reading, to be transported somewhere, or into someone else entirely through the medium of thought.

Eventually the storm eased outside, and Arthur drifted into a contented slumber. The creaking timbers of the bridge were strangely soothing. He was awakened some time later by a strange humming noise from the block instruments. Pushing himself out of the soft chair he walked over to the wall to which they were fastened and noticed the needles jumping erratically. He rubbed the sleep from his eyes and watched as the needles danced, as if drawn by some unstable magnetism. Instantly the humming stopped, and the needles steadied once more. Arthur stroked his beard in thought but could see nothing to explain this phenomenon. He lit his pipe and returned to the chair to consider this occurrence further. No sooner had he sat down, than the humming started again, this time higher pitched and more intense. The needles jumped and bucked in their casings tapping against the glass as if trying to get out! This time the hands of the clock began to spin forward, racing into the future, their motion becoming blurred and unreadable. A shiver ran down Arthur's spine - this was all rather unnerving. Next, he watched astounded as the lever for the home signal started to move in the frame with a slow clicking sound. The scraping metal on metal put his teeth on edge as he grabbed the lever and attempted to force it back into the correct position. It took all his might just to hold it steady and through the window he could see the signal slowly rising to the 'off' position. As he pushed hard on the lever, it pushed back, forcing him to brace himself against the wall. His hands were sweaty, and he soon became breathless with the effort. All of a sudden, the movement and sound stopped, and Arthur lost his footing as he fell forward with the now released lever into the metal frame. Unable to stop himself, he hit his head on the lever and found himself on the floor, blood oozing from his ear and his mind spinning. An almost deathly silence descended. There was no wind and as he lay motionless, he saw white flakes descending in front of the oil lamp outside the box.

He struggled to his feet and peered through the rectangular, uniform windows. Wiping the condensation away, Arthur inspected the signal by the box – horizontally at danger as it should be. He noticed that the snow was beginning to lie, as thick flakes fell, drawing a white blanket over the harbour station. The boats bobbed gently now on the deep black sea, their thick tethers slack in the oily water. He held a rag to his ear to stem the bleeding and winced as he touched his bruised cheek. What had just happened?

As he gazed in contemplation, he noticed movement on the swing bridge. He blinked, trying to make sense of what he was witnessing. Smoke was billowing above the swing bridge and appearing out of the darkness and swathed in steam was a black engine, numbered one-nine-nine. Adrenaline coursed through Arthur's veins and in panic he reached for the emergency lamp and fog signals. Who in God's name was driving that thing and who had given him authority to move that engine? The block instruments again started to whine, and Arthur could only watch as the signal levers began to release from their frames. Instinctively he dashed outside and hurriedly attached fog signals to the railhead as the train bore down on him. Arthur threw himself back from the rail and raised his red lamp to the approaching train. He could see neither driver nor fireman as he shouted "Stop!" from deep in his belly. The detonators exploded beneath the wheels of the engine as sparks flew from the explosion. The tender and coaches passed the desperate signalman, but the train did not appear to be slowing. Arthur jumped onto the empty brake van and frantically applied the brake, but the blocks seemed not to be making contact and slowly, but surely, the speed increased. Arthur felt frozen in time and in terror, desperately trying to work the brakes. He began to realise he was now trapped on a moving train, for he would surely die if he jumped off at this speed. Through the dark night he went, the winter cold biting at him. Time became fluid and though he knew the train must surely stop at the fallen tree that Tommy had warned him of, he saw no sign of it. In fact, he didn't remember

Folkestone Junction at all. Before long he was flying through the Kent countryside, having abandoned all hope of stopping the train.

Night turned to day and it became strangely warm and sunny. In fact, the landscape no longer looked bleak and winter-ridden but inviting like a summer's afternoon. The train rattled on through beautiful countryside, passing by the village of Headcorn and over the clear waters of the River Beult, the Hammer Stream and once more over the Beult, which crisscrossed under the line several times. Suddenly, approaching Staplehurst, the brakes locked on hard and woke Arthur from his daydream. Looking down, he was horrified to see a railway man desperately waving a red flag, his face stricken with terror, his eyes black with fear. Without warning Arthur found he was no longer on the train but standing in a field watching it from a short distance. He could see the track had been lifted over the river. He stood aghast as the train at first straddled the rails miraculously and then jumped across the gap. Like a man unable to stop himself falling, the following coaches slid and crashed their way into the river in the most horrific manner, all bent metal and broken glass. The last first-class coach hung precariously, dangling above the water as it ground to a halt. Arthur was unable to move, utterly dumbstruck, his mouth wide open listening to the cries of the injured. He watched, mesmerised, as someone clambered from the suspended coach. The man had been well dressed but now he stood in tatters catching his breath after the exertion of climbing. He turned his bloodied face to stare directly at Arthur, as he, with utter confusion, recognised a familiar profile. It was none other than his literary hero, Charles Dickens.

Arthur became aware of a strange rattling and then a banging.

"Hey Arthur! Oi, sleepy head!" a gruff voice said through the glass window as he rattled the locked door.

"What? Oh? Er...hold on," said a flustered and flummoxed Arthur. He was in the comfortable armchair in the signal box, and it would appear, he had never left? He opened the door to the fresh morning air and the sound of gulls in the calm after the storm.

"What, did you have one too many last night?" enquired Ron, Arthur's relief.

"No but had the oddest of dreams, you won't believe..." Arthur said, trailing off as once again he felt the bruise on his face.

"Christ's sakes Art, you haven't even boiled the kettle and the fire's out," whined Ron, "You could have at least kept the fire going!" he said, ignoring Arthur's visible distress.

Arthur scowled; he didn't appreciate the Lord's name being taken in vain but, still in shock from the images that seeped into his wakeful consciousness, decided not to argue with Ron. After all, he could not explain with any clarity the events that had taken place that night. He ached as if he were the one involved in a crash and struggled to focus on the train register, which he was required to complete before leaving duty. He checked the time, then checked it again. It was certainly not three thirteen as the railway clock indicated. He looked at his watch - stopped at three thirteen.

"What time do you make it, Ron?" Arthur asked.

Steam rose from the kettle as Ron poured hot water into the pot. Wiping the steam from his glasses, Ron first looked at the inaccurate railway clock then at his watch.

"It's six fifteen. Don't tell me you haven't even wound the clock!" exclaimed the exasperated railwayman.

Arthur quickly opened the glass front and reset the hands of the signal box timepiece. He felt a sudden desire to get away and hurriedly returned to the train register. As he did so, the hairs on the back of his neck stood up, for in the margin of the register, below his last entry, there was written a partial date - 9th June 18... The script was in neither man's handwriting and was just readable, the '8' being smudged across the page as if a hand had been dragged across it. His hand shook as he signed out, trying to ignore this unaccounted entry and turned the page.

For several months Arthur felt haunted by the events of that night and the cries of those injured in the crash stayed with him. As winter turned to spring then to summer, slowly the memory began to fade and become less terrifying. As 9th June approached, the anxiety returned and Arthur suffered a few sleepless nights, but the date passed without incident much to his relief. He was busy at work and outside of it; his life took a turn for the better when he met a lady who would eventually become his wife. He worked hard at the box, keeping the trains moving.

With great pride he accepted his long service award, and, for a time, life was good.

The years passed quickly, and the harbour became increasingly frenetic, becoming the South Eastern Railway Company's principal packet station and gateway to the Continent. Arthur witnessed soldiers heading to the Crimea to fight in that distant war and sadly only some returning. Many prominent statesmen travelled on the trains that he signalled too, although he had little time to rub shoulders with them. And though he looked out keenly for Mr. Dickens, he never did see him. A couple of times, he penned a letter to send to him but as he read it back, he dismissed the idea as madness; the events sounded like pure fiction, a figment of his imagination and the letters remained undelivered in his desk at home.

In 1864, Arthur became one of the most senior signalmen on the railway, second only to Ron by just a few weeks. The relationship between the two men had not improved as Ron became increasingly obstinate and difficult. Luckily, they had no cause to see each other much and Ron was often out of the box before Arthur arrived. Tommy was being trained up to take the reins, always preferring to learn from Arthur and dreading the days he had to spend with Ron, but he was gaining in knowledge and maturity and stuck with it.

Born on New Year's Eve, Arthur always liked to celebrate with a good drink. It had become a tradition to imbibe at The Royal George and then stagger the few hundred yards to the sea, often resulting in an unplanned soaking. As the clock ticked over into 1865, the gathered crowd linked arms and sang into the clear night sky...

"Should all acquaintance be forgot,

For the sake of auld lang syne!"

Arthur didn't feel so good. His legs buckled under him and he remained standing only with the help of the singers either side, with whom he was still linked.

"No swimming for you tonight, Art!" said one of the singers causing a ripple of laughter.

Luckily, home was not too far away, and the revellers happily staggered with him to get him back. He lay in bed with the room spinning and drifted into an uncomfortable dream. Before long, he found himself back in the signal box. The old clock chimed as if it was at the hour, but Arthur could clearly see the time...three thirteen! Again, the box erupted as the levers jolted from the frame and the whole sorry story of the rail crash was yet again recited in his mind. When his wife, Laura, woke him, he was bathed in sweat and not himself. He had not told her about this distressing dream, she assumed it was just over-consumption, but when the nightmare returned for a second and then a third night, Arthur confided a little of the story to her.

Over the coming weeks, Arthur suffered with frequent recurrences, always the same dream, always the same time on the clock and the same engine. Sometimes he felt so rough the day after that he had to go sick, the anxiety making it almost impossible to concentrate. His wife worried for him but had no idea how to help. She did her best to soothe him by wiping the sweat away and bathed his tender face, for the bruise often returned. He was not in his own mind, lost in a black cloud of worry.

After a particularly bad week where he stayed off work, sick, someone from the company came to visit.

"It's like this Arthur," said the well-heeled man, "we simply cannot continue to carry you." The young company representative spoke directly and without compassion. "I am hereby serving notice that if your attendance doesn't improve forthwith, we will have no option but to let you go."

After so many years of service, Arthur was beside himself, reeling from the young man's viciousness. In an attempt to encourage the nightmares to desist, Arthur arranged to do night turns, feeling that if he was awake overnight, they would not come. Unfortunately, the nightmares found their way into his sleep regardless and a few times Arthur made dangerous mistakes at work, for he was exhausted.

One evening in Spring, Arthur was busy as ever when he heard the whistle of an engine outside the box. He slid the window open to speak to the driver and smiled at his good friend, James.

"Hello old timer," said James with typical cockney chirp. "Look at this new beauty I've brought you! Just picked her up from Ashford, ain't she gorgeous?"

The black engine was gleaming as the beautiful sunset reflected off its polished surface.

"I reckon this is the best one yet, goes like a rocket too!" exclaimed James enthusiastically.

"Well I'm sure you'll put her through her paces!" replied Arthur, trying to sound at least half as enthusiastic as his friend.

"Well, I just thought you'd like to meet her," laughed James, giving a loud whistle before releasing the brakes. As the engine trundled slowly past the box, the smile disappeared from Arthur's face, replaced by horror as he noticed the engine number...one-nine-nine. He stared, transfixed, as the steam rose, and the sun dipped below the horizon. The engine was unmistakable, it was the one from his nightmare. From then on, Arthur dreaded seeing that engine. It was a favourite to pull the boat trains to London, along with others of similar design. His troubles continued and sometimes he was unable to attend work. Luckily, Tommy was now almost ready to pass out as a signaller, and people were well used to seeing him working the box. When Arthur couldn't manage it, Tommy would step up and unofficially cover for him. One morning, after working Arthur's shift, he decided to call in to see him at home. It had been a busy night and Tommy had a few questions he needed to ask.

"Morning, Mrs. O'Sullivan," said Tommy as he approached Arthur's house. Mrs. O'Sullivan was busily sweeping the step, a proud housewife. "How's the old man getting on? Is he up?"

"Oh Tommy, it's good of you to drop by, he's really not good, I'm so worried about him." A tear ran down her cheek as she looked to the floor. Tommy put a comforting arm around her. He hadn't had an easy start in life, and Mr. and Mrs. O'Sullivan were like family to him. Tommy went in and climbed the creaky stairs to the bedroom. He knocked on the door, no reply. He knocked again and slowly turned the handle. Arthur was still in bed and looked rough, his face white and his arms thin.

"Hey Arthur, it's me, Tommy." said Tommy, edging closer to the bed.

"Ah Tommy," rasped Arthur, "So good to see you," he said, forcing a thin smile.

"What's the news? I don't even know what day of the week it is!"

Tommy was glad to babble on about work, he hated difficult conversations and the railway was at least safe territory. As the two men talked, Arthur began to feel a little more alive. He liked Tommy and wanted him to do well. He also enjoyed the chance to pass on a lifetime's operational knowledge. The men chatted for a time before Arthur indicated he was tired. Before he left, Tommy reached into his bag and put some papers on the side table,

"I'll leave these here, nothing exciting really but I thought you might want to keep up with developments?"

Arthur nodded his thanks and then nodded off. Tommy left quietly, doffing his cap to Laura as he passed her in the hallway.

"Try not to worry too much, he'll be right as rain in a few weeks, you'll see," said Tommy trying to muster some positivity.

"He won't see a doctor, you know," said Laura gravely. "He needs something to help him sleep."

"Well I can see why he wouldn't want to. Those quacks will sell you anything. But if it helps, I'll ask around for you? Best be off now, Mrs. O'Sullivan and I need some sleep meself."

A day later, Tommy returned with 'medicine'.

"Just make sure he doesn't take too much at once!" said Tommy, handing Mrs. O'Sullivan a brown glass bottle.

"I'm so grateful to you Tommy, you're a good lad." Laura replied with a smile.

The liquid did help calm Arthur down. Sometimes, it knocked him out so at least he could sleep, but he never felt rested. The nightmares didn't stop either. They became jumbled, sometimes playing in reverse, sometimes at double speed, but the details always remained the same.

At around noon on 9th June 1865, Arthur awoke, having slept right through from the night before without dreaming and without a headache. Of course, he wasn't aware of the date or even the day of the week, but at least he felt semi human. Hearing him stir, Laura came upstairs with tea and toast to find an invigorated Arthur shuffling through the papers Tommy had left for him.

At roughly the same time, Mr. Charles Dickens was aboard the ferry bound for Folkestone, having spent a pleasurable month in Paris. He was in good spirits having made excellent progress on his new novel, "Our Mutual Friend." He sat in his cabin making some minor alterations as the steamer made fair progress towards its meeting with the tidal boat train at Folkestone and the subsequent journey to London. As the harbour loomed ever closer, Dickens gathered his belongings and joined his travelling companions, Miss Ellen Ternan and her mother, who were on deck preparing for disembarkation.

As the steamer docked, the driver of the boat train was readying engine No 199 for the journey to London along with the rest of the train crew while the electric telegraph buzzed with communications between the signal boxes clearing the route for the train's departure. Tommy was about to become a qualified signaller, and this was his last shift as understudy of the increasingly disagreeable Ron.

"Come on Tommy, pull your socks up boy, you need to get that route set or you'll delay the train," chided Ron angrily. Tommy swallowed his pride. He was hardly a boy now, but he knew Ron would make life difficult if he answered back. Like the pieces of a puzzle slotting together, the transition from steamer to train was made efficiently and soon it and all its one-hundred-and-fifteen passengers were on their way, passing over the swing bridge and onwards up the hill and out of Folkestone.

Arthur had come downstairs and sat smoking his pipe perusing the working timetable and other railway notices Tommy had delivered. As he sifted through the papers his eyes fell upon the Time Service Table, the working timetable showing when trains were expected to pass certain locations. He had been in such a strange mind of late that he had not realised it was June and the pages showed the workings for Friday 9th and Saturday 10th June 1865. Normally the timings were different being weekday and weekend, but Arthur, accustomed to considering these documents in fine detail, noticed immediately that the 9th and 10th were a perfect match, in other words a duplication. This was highly irregular, especially in terms of the boat train, which, due to the changing tides and the necessity to connect with the steam packet at Folkestone, rarely, if ever, remained the same across any two days. Handwritten and barely legible at the bottom of the page, were the words "Draft: Incorrect - not to be distributed". Arthur's temperature began to rise as he felt a knot tighten in his stomach. He fumbled for another notice, which listed planned works, and with uncontrollable panic, realised what this meant. Work on the 9th was planned at a viaduct crossing the River Beult involving track renewal. If somehow the incorrect workings had found their way into the engineers' hands, then the tragic accident of his nightmares could be real! He grabbed the days morning paper that sat on the side table and he cried out at the date - today was 9th June 1865! He checked his watch and ran to the door...

The journey to London was going well. The train was pretty much on time and it was a blissful day to return to England. Mr. Dickens stood enjoying the fresh Kent air that blew through the open window and realised that although he loved Paris, he much preferred the open countryside of the Garden of England. The train clicked and clacked over the rails and Ellen gazed happily from the train with her window shut as the steam from the engine would almost certainly have covered her in soot. Dickens stood up to admire the view further as they passed the village of Headcorn and the driver began using the whistle.

Arthur puffed along the road and up the steps to the signal box where Ron and Tommy sat, drinking tea. Tommy was happy, Ron had actually praised him for his work that day and allowed him to sit awhile. Usually, he would have been working flat out till the end of his shift.

"Blimey! It's a ghost!" laughed Ron as Arthur burst through the door as if he was about to explode.

"What was the engine number of that tidal train this afternoon?" Arthur spluttered.

"Whoa, hang on. What's this all about?" replied Ron, but Tommy was already at the desk checking the register.

"One-nine-nine," said Tommy with precision. Arthur's eyes widened.

"We must stop that train! Send a message up the line, stop that train!" shouted Arthur who had now worked up a full head of steam.

"Eh? Hang on a minute", said Ron, as he puffed his chest out, "I'm in charge of this box and there ain't no way you're goin' to send a message like that, especially without an explanation. You're not even on duty, you're sick remember, sick in the head."

"There's no time to argue, just send the damn message!" said Arthur as he began to cough. Tommy began to liven up the electric telegraph, the quickest way to pass a message up the line.

"Oh no you don't" said Ron gruffly, pulling Tommy forcefully away from the desk. The two men scuffled and knocked over their tea. Stifling his coughing, Arthur approached the telegraph and began to send an emergency stop message. He looked up nervously as the clock struck three. There was still a chance! Tommy had the upper hand; younger and fitter than Ron, he pushed him onto the floor in the corner of the room, but Ron wasn't finished yet. Arthur received a reply from the next box.

"Emergency stop? For what reason? Please confirm." Exasperated, Arthur tried again.

"Emergency Stop. Line Blocked. Imminent derailment."

As the message chattered its way through the wires, Ron threw a wild punch at Tommy, hitting him squarely in the jaw. Tommy fell backwards, hitting his head on a lever, and knocked himself unconscious.

Meanwhile, the driver of engine one-nine-nine was approaching a signal which was 'off' and in the "proceed" position. As he neared the signal, the driver witnessed the signal drop back to danger. He waited a second. Sometimes, the signalman dropped the wrong signal, maybe it would clear again? But it didn't! In the distance, the driver thought he saw what looked like a red flag waving frantically. He had no choice but to whistle for the brakes to be applied in emergency and the guard did his best to get them on. As the brakes bit, Dickens, who was still standing, admiring the view, had to brace himself as the train slowed sharply under braking. Next, the passengers jumped as detonators exploded beneath the train with a loud bang! As the train came to a standstill with a jolt in the strong summer sunshine, Dickens was not the only one to put his head out of the window to find out what had occurred. The train had left the signal at danger a long way back and running along the track to the driver was a lad with a big red flag, looking very distressed.

"Thank the Lord you stopped!" he cried to the railwaymen.

“What’s the meaning of this?” barked the driver, “Don’t you know this is an express train?”

“Yes Sir, the line’s out ahead. Thank God you stopped, you’d have ended up in the river! We weren’t expecting you for another two hours!”

“Two hours? Don’t you read your notices?” the guard chimed in as the dejected hand signalman dropped his head in disgrace.

“I was just following what the foreman said.” muttered the lad. Dickens looked on, listening to the argument. “Sometimes what happens in real life, is more of a story than I could write,” he thought. He looked across at Ellen. She was beautiful and he was truly grateful that they had not found themselves thrown from the train into a river!

Some days later, Arthur went to see Tommy. This time it was Tommy lying in bed, feeling sorry for himself. Arthur on the other hand, felt better than ever, the dreams no longer bothering him.

“I’ve brought you some pain relief,” he smiled, handing Tommy the brown tincture bottle. The bandage covered half his face and he looked rather comical.

“Well it looks like you don’t need it anymore, old man, you look better than ever.”

Tommy laughed and then immediately winced in pain. “So, what’s the news?”

“Well it seems we’ve been hailed as heroes,” Arthur replied. “They reckon without our actions, that train would have certainly derailed and strangely enough, rather than sacking me, they want to promote me! I expect you’ll get a visit from the company once you feel better, they’re keen to interview you.”

“Well if they ask me anything about that idiot Ron, I’ll tell them straight...”

“Ah don’t worry about him mate, he’s been eating humble pie ever since. He actually asked me to apologise to you.”

“So, will you take a promotion?”

“Well, I might but I think I might have a better offer,” said Arthur as he dropped a rather grand looking letter onto the bed, a glint in his eye. Tommy opened the letter. It was a personal invitation for him to meet with Charles Dickens to discuss the possibilities of a new book, entitled “The Signal-Man”. And so, history was (re)written. Dickens went on to live for another ten years completing “The Signal-Man,” which was a sharp contrast to the one we are familiar with today! The Mystery of Edwin Drood was completed in 1871 to great acclaim and with a killer twist at the end. Arthur O’Sullivan finally lived to see the publication of his own fine volume of railway fiction which he wrote with just a little help from his good friend Charles.

21

The Fossil Hunter

by Nicholas Irwin

It was Friday lunchtime. Oliver was leaning against the red brick wall that surrounded the inner harbour. It was a very familiar scene to him, the old town and the huge incongruous Burstin hotel behind him, the decaying harbour and the distant cliffs of Copt Point in front. He had always thought that this part of town felt rather down at heel but noticed that there was now a steady stream of people crossing the old swing bridge making their way to the new retail developments on the harbour arm. Sailing boats bobbed up and down on the turbid water below him and steel cables clinked rhythmically against aluminium masts. The incoming tide of floating plastic swirled around ropes and rusty girders and a small white rowing boat was in danger of sinking because it had so much rainwater in it. And nearby, too nearby for Oliver's liking, was an opportunist seagull with a razor-sharp beak, edging along the wall towards him with eyes only for his chips.

It must be said that Oliver didn't visit his mother very often. It was quite a journey to Folkestone and somehow life kept on getting in the way. On this occasion, however, Oliver also had a school reunion on the Sunday night, so he had rather run out of excuses not to visit her. As it happened, his mother did not feel neglected at all. She had plenty of friends and everything she needed in her retirement flat in the town centre. For her, playing the neglect card was more for her amusement and gave her a sense of control over a diminishing empire. As he was not expected until dinner time and despite the weather, Oliver had decided to go for a stroll down memory lane, to some of the places he used to visit as a teenager, forty years ago. Just what he needed really, to clear his head from the problems at home.

It had stopped raining and Oliver rolled up his umbrella. But in order to do so he had made the rookie error of putting what remained of his lunch on the wall. Too late. The seagull made its move and a squadron of other gulls swooped in from the rooftops to join the attack. Within ten frenzied seconds the food and the box it came in had gone, leaving splinters of polystyrene all over the pavement. Oliver swiped his umbrella at the gulls as he set off towards the disused railway bridge and the cobbled quay beyond.

On the quay, tough looking fishermen with leathery faces were busy unloading their catches from the fishing boats in plastic trays. The gutting shed was closed. Oliver was rather disappointed because he and his friend Daniel used to enjoy watching the fish being gutted, cool steel blades slicing through tough skin, before gloved hands pulled out strings of throbbing gut from still-wriggling bellies and dropping them into metal buckets. Oliver continued his walk along the quay, past the sea food market and Ship Inn towards Coronation Parade and his destination beyond.

Coronation Parade was a concrete structure that consisted of a long series of interconnecting chambers. It held the sandstone cliffs behind it in check and provided a path on top, all the way to the rocks at Copt Point. One of Oliver's earliest memories was getting lost in those chambers. He had wandered off the crowded beach to go exploring and became disorientated. Oliver still remembered the terror of the chambers, for each looked exactly the same, dark, threatening, and offering no reference point whatsoever for him to retrace his steps. He was eventually rescued by two big girls and returned to his mother in floods of tears.

The sandy beach below the Parade was now under water, the tide having forced families to take to the nearby cafes and amusement arcades, still clutching their buckets and spades. As an amusing distraction, Oliver decided today to walk through all those interconnecting chambers, but he soon regretted his decision, as the concrete floor was very slippery, and he was only wearing lightweight shoes. And although those childhood terrors could now be dismissed with a bit of adult reasoning, he still felt distinctly disturbed as he walked from one chamber to the next. He subconsciously hastened his steps, passing a confused crab here and there, some mussels clinging gamely to the concrete walls, and two large catfish that had been thrown up by the waves, decomposing underneath a shawl of flies. At the end of the Parade Oliver finally climbed up some steps to bring him back to the path above him. He then went through the railings, ignoring the warning notices of unstable cliffs (like everybody did) and made his way slowly over the jumbled rocks and seaweed towards Copt Point.

Oliver remembered that this part of the journey was always difficult because the sandstone rocks at the foot of the cliffs had sharp edges and slimy green faces. Today the high tide made things particularly difficult and there was not much room in which to manoeuvre between land and sea. Oliver kept sliding into rock pools and cursed his choice of footwear. Eventually he reached the sewage outfall at Copt Point. This was where the cliffs turned from sandstone to the highly fossiliferous gault clay, and this was where he and his friend Daniel used to hunt for fossils.

Oliver had been introduced to fossils by his father on a family holiday to Dorset. Over the years he had found bivalves and brachiopods, ammonites and belemnites, gastropods and sea urchins, worms, shark teeth and pieces of fossilised wood. One of his most prized was the vertebra of a plesiosaur although to many people the little lump of stone could have been anything. Oliver was pleased to be back again. Nothing much had changed although the ferries no longer came by. The waves continued to break over the rocks, agitated seagulls fought in the sky above, and the clay cliffs continued to slip into the sea.

Oliver started to climb up the cliff face. The clay crumbled away in his hands and stuck to his shoes in balls. He pulled out the larger pieces of clay and carefully examined them before letting them cartwheel down to the beach. This would normally present some danger to people below him, but he had assumed that he was alone. However, this was not the case because, quite suddenly, a young man appeared on the beach down below, crouching over a rock pool. Oliver immediately stopped and shouted "Sorry" down to him but was unsure whether he had been heard. Oliver continued to work his way methodically eastwards into Wear Bay where the sight of the white cliffs of Dover never failed to impress him. The rain had started to fall again now, and a mist was rolling in from the sea. He was just about to return to the beach when he noticed a glimmer in the cliff face. Standing precariously on a ledge he was just able to loosen the material around it and prise the fossil out of its snug clay bed. A thin but complete pyritised ammonite was now lying in his hands, about three inches in diameter, and even bigger and more beautiful than the one that was universally admired when Daniel took his fossil collection into school. "Anahoplites planus," he said to himself proudly and carefully placed the fossil in his rucksack.

As he descended the cliff, Oliver could again see the boy below him, turning over rocks at the bottom of the cliff. The boy did not look up as Oliver approached but something made Oliver stop short. There was nothing particularly unusual about the boy except that he was wearing flares, but Oliver reminded himself that, inexplicably, flares had made something of a comeback recently. Oliver reckoned that the boy was about 20 years old. He was quite tall in stature, unshaven and had long unruly ginger hair that hung down to his narrow shoulders and partially covered his face. He was also wearing trainers and a scruffy Stranglers T shirt and didn't appear to have a coat. Oliver's thought at that moment, and one that would eventually haunt him for the rest of his life, was how much the boy resembled the Daniel he used to know some forty years ago. The Stranglers T shirt clinched it. They were his favourite band and he and the T shirt were considered inseparable.

"Hello," said Oliver brightly but there was no response. The boy did not make eye contact and continued slowly turning over the pebbles. Every now and again he would pick something up, examine it and then discard it. "Found anything?" added Oliver, assuming he had met a fellow fossil collector. The boy remained silent. For a second Oliver thought the boy might be deaf.

"I wondered when you would come," said the boy eventually in a soft voice.

This one comment stumped Oliver and it took him a little while to respond to it. And during those moments he felt that time stood still, being caught halfway between the past and the present. Eventually the present reasserted itself, and Oliver decided that the boy might have special needs. Indeed, he expected a parent or older brother, or perhaps even a carer to appear from around the corner. But nobody appeared.

"Don't you have a coat?" asked Oliver at last. It was raining quite hard by now.

"You need to mind the cliffs," said the boy.

"I'm fine, thanks," said Oliver "I know this place well"

In the absence of a guardian, Oliver started to feel responsible for the boy. It was like finding a stray dog. And the boy projected a vulnerability that prevented Oliver from just walking off. He needed to reassure himself that the boy could be safely left behind.

The boy continued to dig around in the rock pool but when he finally got up and moved to another pool it was obvious that he had a limp. And that shocked Oliver because Daniel also had a limp, a legacy of childhood polio.

"Have you hurt yourself?" asked Oliver but he again got no answer. The boy turned to go, his hand covering one side of his face. "My name is Oliver," said Oliver, making a final attempt at conversation, and expecting the boy to reciprocate as is convention, but no name was forthcoming.

His decision to make the boy safe was rather taken out of Oliver's hands because the boy suddenly got up and limped off towards the harbour, scrabbling over the rocks at considerable speed. Oliver watched him go around the headland until the mist made it impossible to see him anymore.

*

Oliver arrived at the school at half past six that Sunday evening. He was half an hour early and found himself a seat in the cemetery opposite. It was strange that the cemetery was still open, but he was grateful that he could sit alone and have a cigarette before the reunion began. A strange feeling of impending doom had come over him which he had put down to nerves. The truth is he was rather shaken up by the boy he had met at Copt Point and could not get the image out of his head. Oliver braced himself for the evening ahead and hoped to avoid the embarrassment of not recognising fellow pupils or worse, they not recognising him. The trouble with this reunion, thought Oliver, was that it was for all pupils that had attended the school in the 1970s, not just his year. A themed evening (including photographs of famous footballers and politicians, vol au vents and a glam rock soundtrack) was all very well but it meant that Oliver had to go and find his old class mates from a crowd of essentially strangers.

At the entrance to the school was a very efficient lady ticking off the arrivals on her notepad. Oliver joined the queue and noticed that she had a huge bust and a rather squeaky voice. He assumed that the lady with the notepad was the school secretary. A badge pinned to her chest confirmed it. "Ms Tye, School Secretary," it said.

"Name please" asked Ms Tye officiously.

"Oliver Smith," said Oliver.

"This is your name badge," said Ms Tye, handing him a piece of plastic bearing the legend "Oliver Smith 1970-1977." There was something resembling a smile on her face.

Oliver followed the crowds down the endless dusty corridors (which he only partly remembered) until he finally reached the assembly hall (which had only just been built). A confident man would have just walked in to the assembly hall and spoken to the first person he met. Oliver was not such a man. He entered the room with his head lowered in nervous anticipation. This probably explained why the first thing he noticed was the slippery floor and the markings of a basketball court. When he did look up Oliver saw a large number of people in huddled groups dotted around the hall. He estimated that there were over two hundred people there. Swirling around the groups were a sea of bewildered faces, just like his own, the unfortunate people, those that had yet to find an appropriate group to join...

At this point Mr Long, the headmaster, entered the room. Oliver could immediately tell it was the headmaster because he had the quick stride and nervous energy that all headmasters seem to have, all smiles and deference to grown-ups, and frowns and condescension to the pupils. Well, as Oliver qualified as grown up (he was sixty-one years old) he expected deference at least.

The Hall went quiet and Mr Long introduced himself before launching into the predictable preliminary that is readily exchangeable with any social occasion: "Thank you for coming" "It's a pleasure to see so many people" "Many have travelled a long way" etc. Mr Long went through the usual housekeeping information, pointing out the fire escapes and the toilets. Oliver noted his best escape route.

Rather predictably, Mr Long went on at some length about how successful the school had become (Ofsted described the school as "excellent") and how brilliant his teachers were, not to mention the invaluable support of the teaching assistants. "We didn't have teaching assistants in our day" said a man next to Oliver with an ill-fitting suit. "Those were the days when a good teacher could hold the attention of 30 pupils and still have time to nip outside for a fag."

"We are committed to providing value for money, we are committed to excellence, and we are committed to diversity, and health and safety, and to reducing waste," Mr Long continued like a primed robot. "We are disability friendly, we have zero tolerance of bullying and parental aggression…." Oliver wondered whether all the effort to make the school politically correct had actually left any time for teaching. Mr Long ended his speech by thanking the school secretary who had organised the event, and the small band of volunteers who had provided the food and drinks. Ms Tye blushed with the applause.

"As you can imagine," Mr Long went on, "it does cost the Friends of the School money to run events such as this. I suggest a donation of £40 per head would be appropriate. If you would just go and see our secretary Ms Tye, at the door...I hope you have a good evening," he concluded, before striding through a fire escape at the back of the Hall and disappearing, like a magician.

Oliver went off to pay Ms Tye. She was now blocking a door with her chest. Oliver decided it must have been an occupational hazard for her. He gave her £20 and she frowned at him. "I will put that in the safe," she said, with more than a hint of sarcasm in her voice. "Perhaps you would like to donate to the school regularly?" She handed Oliver a form. "It's a direct debit mandate. And tax efficient". Oliver took the form and shoved it into his jacket pocket.

Oliver did eventually find a few friends he knew: Neil had discussed green field development, and Andrew discussed his inability to find a wife (have mine, said Joey). Then there was Mark, recounting tedious stories to illustrate his son's academic prowess at Cambridge, and Martin, who only wanted to talk about football. After an hour of this Oliver went outside for a cigarette. When he returned to the Hall, he noticed a man sitting in a corner alone, ploughing his way through piles of sandwiches. Oliver hadn't recognised him because he had lost his mop of curly brown hair and had put on a lot of weight. His badge said: 'Roger Pope 1970-1977."

"Roger!" exclaimed Oliver. Roger looked at him suspiciously at first until he had read and assimilated the information on Oliver's badge. "Oliver!" cried Roger, standing up to offer a large pink hand to shake in a cloud of breadcrumbs.

Roger was probably the largest man Oliver had ever seen, with an enormous belly that had won the fight with the buttons on his blue suit some years ago. He wore brown shoes and silver cuff links, little mermaids with giant breasts. His face was puffy and jovial whilst his bald head shone under the bright lights of the Hall. They went to the makeshift bar to get a soft drink and then returned to the food. Oliver filled up his little disposable plate with a sausage roll, some chicken on skewers and some coleslaw. Roger filled up three plates with sandwiches. He moved towards the main window and Oliver followed him. Oliver soon realised that Roger had moved there to ogle the school secretary.

Roger still lived locally. Apart from their both being married and each having two children, Oliver realised that they had very little in common. And when Oliver said that he was retired Roger appeared completely disinterested. That was quite a common reaction. It seemed to Oliver that people define you by your job. If you didn't have a job, there was little to talk about. Roger was much happier talking about his own career anyway and Oliver allowed him to do so. He did have a whole evening to kill, after all. Roger explained that he was a family liaison officer, providing a sort of buffer between the offender, the police, the courts, and the offender's family.

"I bet that is stressful," said Oliver.

"It takes a special kind of person to do it" said Roger, self-importantly.

The conversation was punctuated by pregnant pauses and awkward silences. "I thought we might have been offered something a little more substantial than a sandwich tonight," Oliver said at last.

"A sandwich can never be anything other than substantial!" snapped Roger as he crammed his mouth with ham and mustard. "You can eat your pretentious sushi, falafels and duck wraps if you like, but people will consider you foreign and laugh at you". Oliver noticed a lump of Branston pickle on Roger's tie making a perilous journey towards his groin. Oliver pointed it out to his friend, and he flicked it on to the floor.

"Have you remained in touch with..." Oliver asked, but Roger interrupted him. "Of course, you might think bringing mixed salads to work in little Tupperware containers make you appear healthy and attractive" said Roger "but you would be deluded. In fact, all other choices just shout one thing - Loser". "Did you know that a sandwich becomes more delicious the further it is from the place that it was made?" he asked, "and that there is no relationship between your appetite and the size of your lunch box?" Roger sniggered. "In fact," he continued "it would not be exaggerating to say that the first mouthful of a sandwich is much like scoring the winning goal in a cup final. Or like an orgasm."

"Quite right," said Oliver, trying to get the image of Roger having an orgasm out of his head.

Martin had joined them at this point. "Talking of cup finals..." he said but Roger interrupted him. "I need to syphon the python," he announced in a loud voice. When he returned, he found Martin and Oliver discussing former class mates. "Peter Cox died of cancer a few years back," Martin was saying "and Phil Jackman died in a car accident".

"Then there was Simon Perry," added Roger. "He also had cancer"

"Peter White," said Martin "He had a heart attack"

The roll call of the Fallen went on.

"John Webb" said Roger. "He was permanently sectioned. I don't know if he is still alive"

"Marcus Eaton," said Martin "is now in a wheelchair"

Oliver had been waiting patiently to ask his question. It had to be asked, given what he had experienced at Copt Point.

"What happened to Daniel Moreton? he finally said.

"Quasimodo?" said Martin. "The guy with the limp?"

"Yes," said Oliver.

"He committed suicide" said Martin. "It was only a couple of years after our A levels" he added.

Oliver felt sick. "How did he die?" he asked when he had sufficiently recovered his composure

"I think he hanged himself" said Martin.

"In Folkestone?" asked Oliver

"I can't remember," said Martin.

Oliver began to relax again though he was sad that his old mate Daniel was no longer alive.

"Whilst we are on the subject of death," said Martin turning towards Roger, "have the police identified the young lad they found at Copt Point yesterday?"

The question hit Oliver hard. No sooner had he dealt with one death, another one threatened to engulf him. And he became overwhelmed with guilt for not doing more for the boy when he encountered him on the beach.

"No identification yet," said Roger. "One of my mates in the police force told me yesterday that, apart from his Stranglers T shirt, there was little left of him. Maybe the gulls ate him."

"I heard that his head was missing," Martin added helpfully

“Well I don’t know about that,” said Roger. “But, unsurprisingly, I did hear that the death was being treated as suspicious. The police said the body had been there for weeks,” he added.

Oliver sat down on a chair. He was overwhelmed as he tried to make sense of it all and he tried not to show it. He was surprised that he had not found the body himself. “Been there for weeks,” he murmured to himself. There was relief in that. But he needed to get his head around everything else. One ghost? Two ghosts?

It was time for a stiff drink.

22

Weather is a Third to Place and Time

by A L Marchant

Ben was drunk to begin with. Christmas drunk. A light buzz in his head from some seasonal drinkies with workmates had swelled, like the storm outside, to a maelstrom.

He slurred his goodbyes and stepped from the relative warmth of the bar into the cold, wet beyond. It was then that some part of his brain suggested to his legs that they stroll home along the seafront. Something about listening to the rhythmic breathing of the waves soothed him.

The rain didn't bother him. That too was refreshing, and he slowly, staggeringly stumbled past the damp woollen poppies of the Road of Remembrance to the beach below.

The vast, white spectre-like bulk of the Burstin motel moved past him as Ben dragged his feet forward, and soon enough he felt the crunch of pebbles beneath his feet. He stood beneath the bell on the stony beach and strained to hear it sing out in the dark.

Watching the sea as well as he could through water-lashed eyes, for a moment it seemed that it was rising to meet him -to consume him – that the previously reassuring sighs were now low growls turning to roars, and that the sea had become a leviathan.

Unthinking, he found himself screaming in defiance "WHO ARE YA!" and rocked unsteadily in soaked shoes, laughing in genuine amusement at his own drunkenness.

He turned, and was about to turn and set off home, when he saw the figure.

A lone figure.

Stood knee deep in the water. Quite still. Quite impassive to the current as it moved about them.

Ben, overcome by a surge of adrenaline, rushed slapdash over the stones, falling and racing down to the shadowed form.

Yet, once at the water's edge, Ben could not bring himself to go further. In his defence, the figure was hardly struggling. It just stood there as before, not calling out, not flailing in desperation. The only thing Ben could identify about it was its stillness.

"Hey!" he called out. "Hey! Are you all right?"

The figure neither spoke nor moved.

"You should get out of there. You'll get hypothermia or something."

The figure neither moved nor spoke.

"You're not -you know- trying to top yourself or something. Because...well, you shouldn't."

The rain was doing its best to blind Ben, but it did seem to him as if the figure shook his head.

"Look," he implored. "It's pissing it down out there. I really think you should get out. If you've got no money or whatever, I'll shout you a coffee at McDonald's or something.

A voice, either from the figure or the back of Ben's mind, intoned:

"Weather is a third to place and time."

Up above, a cloud shifted, a storm paused, time slowed, and the moon illuminated the world.

The figure was russet and metal, inhuman and naked. Unreal. Ben had seen it before. A statue that usually stood vigilant beneath the Harbour Arm.

He had often felt sorry for it, despite it being an unliving thing. Forever frozen. Forever staring at the tide as it rose and fell around it. Forever nearly drowning, every day. What must it have seen as time had passed? What might it see as days went by? Watching the world all alone from its lonely platform.

Why should it care about the rain then?

But why was it here?

How was it here?

Suddenly, silently, the statue turned and faced Ben. Time returned. The storm returned. The clouds returned. The dark returned. And the statue started slowly towards Ben.

Ben backed away, terrified. Somehow, he did not know why, he was standing knee deep in the sea. As the figure lurched close, he tried to turn but fell face down in the surf. He scrabbled to his feet, swallowing and retching the salty water, wiping his eyes with his sleeve to see the safe land ahead of him.

Then, the statue stepped into his view.

None of Ben's work colleagues were sure what had happened to him when they got back into the office in the New Year. Some remembered him saying that he was going to see family in Exeter. From that, others assumed that he had decided to stay there. And from that assumption, more pointed out that he never seemed particularly happy at the firm. And so, life went on.

And out there, by the pebbly beach, people out for a peaceful walk along the seaside began to remark what a nice surprise it was that they had added a second statue to that platform beneath the harbour arm, and how nice it was that they were holding hands.

23

Words of Comfort

by

Deborah J Jones, Jane Cottle and Suzannah Gisby

Alfred checked himself in the gilt mirror in the servants' corridor before taking up his station in the lift. Tie straight, buttons on his livery jacket done up properly, shoes polished, hair combed neatly; he would do. Times changed at the Grand Hotel; ladies' skirts grew shorter, then longer, and shorter again. Musical tastes changed too. There were no longer any dances on the sprung dance floor; the vibrations upset the residents in the apartments upstairs. Rather a shame, he thought. Sometimes he would execute a little twirl on there, on a quiet evening, imagining the band playing some of the tunes his old Mum and Dad had loved to listen to on the wireless.

"Night and day," he sang to himself.

Structurally, things had changed somewhat. The reception area had moved – overall, a good thing, he thought. Yet his mirror remained the same – it had survived the war, with just a few tiny marks – and Alfred would forever be fifteen years old. In fact, he had not left the hotel since that terrible day all those years ago, when the lift had stuck, then come loose from its moorings (he was taking two enormous cabin trunks up to the fourth floor) and plunged him down, down, down into the basement with a crash and a sickening screech, followed by blackness.

He had watched himself being taken out by the undertaker on a stretcher. He had stretched his hands out to Mum and Dad and tried to say something, but no words came out. They both just cried, following mutely behind the lugubrious men in black, wrapped up in grief. They didn't seem to realise he was there at all. He'd wished and wished for them to turn around, but they hadn't. He had looked out for them for years and for his little brother and sister too but there hadn't been any sign. Not knowing quite what to do with himself, he had simply returned to his duties.

"Evening, Mr Ashby." He greeted the staff manager politely, but there was no reaction. He tried again; still nothing. Standing in the corridor by the lift and feeling rather daring, he made a face at the manager's ramrod straight departing back but there was no reaction. Some people knew he was there, some felt a presence (a friendly, slightly mischievous one, they reported.) Another thing which was different was the guest lift; modern and not nearly as imposing now, but Alfred had soon got to grips with it. They'd taken the service lift out of commission, but he could still make it go up and down. Guests on the third and fourth floor often reported the clunking sound of a lift and the eerie noise of a bell.

Alfred soon worked out that some people could see him, but others could not. There seemed to be no rhyme or reason for that. He had also worked out that he could go backwards as well as forwards in time. One afternoon, he had wandered into what looked like a hospital ward, but which was actually one of the upstairs reception rooms. He wondered what the housekeeper would have made of the chaos and the smell. He'd recognised his own family doctor – a younger and less portly version, who addressed him directly and in hurried tones.

"Don't just stand there, young man; make yourself useful. Boatful of Canadians just come in from the Front. All hands to the pump."

Alfred had found himself perched on a chair beside a camp bed, next to a young soldier with a stump for a leg, pale with dark eyes which seemed too large for his face.

"You'll be fine, mate. You'll get home to Canada and you'll be right as rain. Say hello to my Auntie Lil for me, won't you? She lives in Esquimalt – sounds like Eskimo. Do you know it?"

But the soldier didn't seem to see him or hear him; his hand shook as he lit himself a cigarette. Alfred wished he could hold the match steady for him, but he couldn't always make things work. Not reliably, anyway; lift buttons were a different matter.

"I'd better get on." Alfred stood up to take his leave. The floor shook underneath his feet. Actually, the whole hotel seemed to be rocking on its foundations. The big guns from the Western front; his grandma Eliza had talked about that, said it was enough to drive anyone mad. She'd come to live with them in Black Bull Road when she became elderly and infirm; took to her bed upstairs, with a commode next to it. That hadn't been at all pleasant, but he did miss their chats.

In pensive mood, Alfred summoned the lift. If he really concentrated hard, he could get back to the late thirties, although he couldn't always be specific and usually tried to avoid the time around the accident.

"Oh, here comes trouble." Alfred's passenger sat down heavily on the narrow, hard bench.

"Afternoon, Mrs Taufflieb. How was America?"

"New York? Fine, thank you, Alfred. But there's less and less to keep me there, and too many memories. I'm looking forward to getting back to Cannes now."

In his mind's eye, Alfred could picture the places she described. The luggage label on her trunk said: "Villa Nevada, Cannes." He'd seen the posters advertising the Golden Arrow train to Paris and the steamers to New York. He'd never even been as far as London, but he did like hearing about her adventures. She had told him about her little girl, who had died in a horrific accident, falling through a plate glass skylight. He didn't like to dwell on that, and would urge her instead to talk about Rudyard Kipling, her friend for many years. At St Mary's School, he had won a copy of the Jungle Book for neat handwriting and he had treasured it. He hoped his brother and sister were being careful with it.

"Do you think I'll ever go back to America, Alfred?"

Alfred could see jumbled pictures, aeroplanes, and smoke, grey uniforms, a journey over mountains into a warm, sunny country and another boat. She would get to America all right, but it probably wouldn't be easy.

"I'm sure you will, Mrs T." He opened the gate for her. "Take care now."

Conversations he overheard and newspapers he craned his neck to make out told him of another war, one in which he would, he supposed, have fought, had things been different, and one in which civilians played a far greater role. He'd heard about bombs being dropped near Black Bull Road. He hoped everyone at number 24 would be safe.

His passenger safely installed in her suite on the fourth floor (with a view of the Channel,) Alfred wandered along the corridor to the service lift. He wondered if standards might slip in this new conflagration as he overheard two chambermaids talking about joining up, getting out of this dump. He'd heard the Grand described as many things but never as a dump. That sounded depressing. Thoughtfully, he pushed the button to take him downstairs to the kitchen. A more modern, cheerful era would be just the ticket.

"Hello," Alfred thought. "Christmas already?"

It looked like it. The staff, several of whom were wearing paper hats and tinsel crowns, were preparing dinner. Some of them were singing along to John Lennon on the radio. "Happy Christmas." Alfred joined in, softly. He liked his music and particularly this song. He had seen the magazines the girls brought into work sometimes. He couldn't for the life of him understand why someone would want to wear his hair long like that though. He wandered up to the next floor and found himself standing beside a young chap in the staff corridor. He knew him – name was Ahmed.

"All right, mate?" Ahmed came from a place called Syria. Alfred didn't know much about Syria, although he always used to like the Sunday school teacher showing them the pictures of the Holy Land in the Bible. Perhaps it was like that. He also remembered a hymn they used to belt out in church:

"In simple trust, like theirs who heard,

Beside the Syrian sea"

He'd loved that one.

Ahmed was a nice fellow and liked to talk. His English was getting better. He worried about his family at home, he told Alfred. Alfred knew exactly what that was like. He put a friendly hand on Ahmed's shoulder. Ahmed didn't seem to mind at all.

"Look after yourself," he called to Ahmed, who had come to the end of his shift and was on his way out of the side door, pulling his thin jacket on, shivering in anticipation of a long walk home, with a cold wind blowing from the East. Over Ahmed's shoulder, Alfred could see the crisp frost on the Leas and the reflection of the moon on the dark sea.

Alfred noticed one of the new young managers, Carlos, striding through Reception, hoping to catch Ahmed. He was from Spain. Now that was somewhere Alfred knew a little more about. One of his Dad's workmates from the Gas Company had gone out there, to fight against Franco. He wasn't sure whether the man ever made it back to Folkestone; he never heard the end of the story. He liked Carlos, although he never seemed to notice him.

"It's late, Ahmed," Carlos said, "And it's cold and you have an early start tomorrow. Why don't you stay upstairs in one of the staff rooms?"

Ahmed accepted gratefully. Alfred nodded approvingly. Sometimes, on a cold winter's night, Mr Ashby had let him do the same, and he had been glad to climb, bone tired, up the last couple of flights, into one of the little attic rooms. That's where Mum and Dad thought he was at first, safely tucked up in bed, when it happened, when he hadn't come home.

Alfred's attention was caught by a man standing impatiently by Carlos's desk, drumming his fingers, waiting for the manager to stop talking to Ahmed. Cedric Hazard, that was his name. He had seen him before, on the television in Mrs T's old suite (he still thought of it as hers.) He could remember when the first television arrived at the Grand and all the excitement that had caused in the residents' lounge. Now there was a television in each bedroom. Probably a good idea, Alfred thought; saved all the arguments. This cove though reminded him, in a funny sort of way, whenever he'd seen him on television, of going to see the Pathé news at the cinema as a youngster - biplanes overhead, tanks, torches, serried ranks of soldiers and harsh, guttural German. His Dad had always been in a bad mood afterwards.

Ahmed made his way to the lift and, after a moment, the man followed. He gave Ahmed an ill-natured stare and then looked down at his mobile. He swore softly when he saw that it was out of charge. That was something else that interested Alfred; people carrying telephones around with them. He had noticed how, over the years, they had become smaller but nonetheless more than just telephones and how they seemed to absorb their users. It seemed rather rude.

"Fourth floor, Mr Hazard?" Alfred asked politely. The three of them had all stepped into the old lift, exactly as it was in the thirties. Mrs Taufflieb's walking stick was propped in the corner. Sometimes, time and space became all muddled up. Tonight was probably going to be one of those nights. No matter; Alfred was a skilled operator. Cedric looked at him curiously and nodded. Alfred closed the door and drew the iron gate across.

The lift creaked and grumbled as it made its way up to the top. Alfred jabbed at the buttons when they reached the fourth floor, but it didn't stop and suddenly shot downwards. Alfred continued jabbing. This was exactly what had happened before but this time he was ready, when it juddered to a halt between the second and the third floors. If only he'd had Mrs T's walking stick with him then! With strength he didn't know he still possessed, he wrenched the outer door open and jammed the walking stick through the iron bars. The lift rocked gently for a moment and then stopped.

"There." He turned to reassure his companions, remembering how terrified he had felt. "We won't be going nowhere now. They'll get us out of here in a jiffy, don't you fret."

"Look, I don't know who the hell you think you are or what you think you're doing," Cedric began. "But I need to get to my room. I have a conference call at midnight." He shot a further dirty look at Ahmed and continued: "About migrants."

Alfred had no idea what he meant or indeed why anyone in their right mind would be at a conference at midnight at this time of year. The man was clearly insane. He didn't look well either. He was sweating profusely and had gone pale. He sank down onto the hard bench beside Alfred, his head in his hands. Ahmed took a bottle of water out of his backpack.

"This might help," he suggested. After a moment, Cedric accepted it.

"Thank you." He looked at Ahmed and added "*Shukrun.*"

Alfred was impressed. That, whatever it meant, seemed to have broken the ice. He listened, fascinated, as Cedric talked to Ahmed about his army training and his time in Iraq and Ahmed spoke of his medical studies, which were on hold for a while. They all told the daftest jokes they could remember. Some of them were quite rude. Alfred chatted too. He was good at that; anything that came into his head. He tried to join in with the chat about football, but he couldn't remember the players. He could remember some great games when he was a youngster though, so he talked about them. He talked about 24 Black Bull Road too, and the cosy kitchen and the Christmas tree they put up – only on Christmas Eve, mind – in the front parlour, a room they rarely used but it did look lovely.

Alfred was just describing opening his presents with his brothers and sisters, only after church of course, and remembering what he'd got that last Christmas and how, with his earnings, he'd bought Mum some handkerchiefs, when the lift began to move again, the gears clanking and whirring, and deposited them all safely on the ground floor, near reception. He watched as Ahmed and Cedric climbed out, to be greeted by a relieved Carlos and the hotel maintenance crew.

"Good luck with your studies," Cedric called to Ahmed. "Hope all goes well." To Carlos he commented "Do pass on my thanks to your lift attendant. A very personable young man."

Alfred chuckled as he watched Carlos's expression. Then, a young couple caught his eye, hovering beside the large, beautifully decorated Christmas tree in the lobby. He had seen them around, heard them bickering. The lady had lost a baby recently. She looked exhausted – peaky, his mother would have said. The pale glow from the lights didn't do her complexion any favours.

"It'll be fine, you'll see," Alfred reassured her with a smile. She smiled back and turned to her husband.

"Let's go for a walk," she suggested. "Tomorrow's Christmas day after all."

"Why not? Best wrap up warm though."

Alfred watched the husband tuck a scarf around her, with a tender gesture.

"That's better," he thought.

Back in the old service lift, Alfred studied the panel. "Where to now?" he wondered. "Pot luck, I suppose."

The lift began a slow descent into the kitchen. He could hear his parents' voices. "Come on, Alfred!" Once or twice, before the accident, especially when he'd just started the job and was learning the ropes, they'd come to collect him, and Mr Ashby used to let them wait in the kitchen for his shift to finish. And now, here they were again, at last. He was about to say; "You took your time," but instead, he called "Wait for me! I'm coming" and he stepped out of the lift into his Mum's embrace. In her good coat and wearing a splash of that perfume he liked (he could picture it on her dressing table now, in a bottle with a pump which his little sister always loved to play with) she didn't look a day older.

Then again, he thought, as he linked arms with his parents, "Why would she?"

"Night, Mr Ashby," he called.

"Goodnight son," came the reply. "Safe journey home."

"I've had the great pleasure of meeting the members of Write by the Sea, so I'm thrilled to find such varied work from its talented writers in this wonderful anthology."
Julie Wassmer (author of The Whitstable Pearl Mysteries)
Karen Marwood
A L Marchant
Deborah J Jones
Tony Quarrington
Jane Cottle
Mark Brophy
Jana Chatters
Paul W Robinson
Lynzy Heartfield
Nick Irwin
Carol Grimes
Tony Hulse
Aleksandra Michalska
Andrew Paul
Carol Harte
Margaret Harland-Suddes
Chani Barnes
Mary Leadbetter
Suzannah Gisby
WRITE BY THE SEA - DECEMBER 2020

Biographies

Carol Grimes

Singing for her supper since the late 1960s, having started out as a nervous busker and having fallen in love with singing. Over time, Carol became a singer songwriter, performance poet, voice movement therapist and musical director. She founded and for many years directed the Sing for Joy Choirs in London. She has recorded and performed in the UK and internationally and has performed at the Albert Hall in the Proms as a soloist.

Carol's first book, The Singer's Tale, was published in 2018 and she has published, recorded and performed many songs and poems over the years. She loves writing as much as she loves music. For more information, check out www.carolgrimes.com.

Jane Cottle

Retired teacher and has lived around Folkestone since 2003. Jane has always enjoyed making up stories and remembers, at the age of around nine or ten, telling her teacher that she would be a writer when she grew up. She loves singing and acting and has written and produced several school plays and musicals – writing the songs as well – and has written articles for local newspapers and academic texts.

As a teacher of the blind, Jane's main teaching resource has been words and being able to describe the world to students who have never experienced vision. She can also read and write in Braille.

Deborah J Jones

Genealogist and editor; has run her own business since 2004. Before that, following a degree in Law and French at the University of Sussex, she worked for the European Union in Brussels as a graduate trainee. She then worked for Lloyd's of London on the scandals that rocked the City in the eighties and for a Private Investigator business with its headquarters in Washington DC.

Deborah is the co-author, under the pen name D A Kent, of Dateline Haifa, published in 2019. More information can be found on Facebook - @TheClementsChronicles – and Deborah can be contacted via gorddinan@live.com.

Karen Marwood

Writes a daily post on her lifestyle blog at https://karensworld-writer.co.uk. Writing about her town, Folkestone, with reviews of places and local authors, keeps her busy. Karen has written many short stories which have featured in other Folkestone anthologies. When she isn't writing, Karen's favourite place to be is her garden with a book. Her first book, "Broken Daughter," which is a memoir, is to be published next year. Karen has three children and ten grandchildren, who all live locally.

Karen started Write by the Sea (find out more on https://folkestonewritebythesea.wordpress.com) last year, as she felt Folkestone needed to pull together all the different aspects of creating a book. It has gone from strength to strength, gaining new members constantly. This anthology is the first publication for Write by the Sea. Contact her on karensworld.writer@yahoo.com.

Carol Harte
Compassionate individual with a strong imagination reflected in her stories, which are packed with interesting facts and observations, gained throughout her travels as a young woman, speckled with aspects of an interesting career as a secretary, teacher of office skills and as an HR professional. Carol enjoys writing and has published "Celia's Retaliation," a spy and romantic thriller, on amazon. Contact her on carol@alteredfuture.co.uk.

Lynzy Heartfield
Lived in Cornwall for twenty years, looking after people with learning disabilities in her own guest house Gannet House, for nearly ten years. She has accumulated qualifications in art and design over the years as an interest, which has helped her in producing her own character illustrations for the mini-series she is writing, called On the Marsh. She has set herself a challenge of writing six books; not bad for a sixty-one-year-old.
Contact her on lynda.marie.goodier@btinternet.com.

Andrew Paul
Researcher, lyricist and singer, and the author of Rue Bonaparte, published in 2014. He is the co-author, under the name D A Kent, of Dateline Haifa which was published in 2019. He has two more books coming out soon - F'Puss in Paris (to be published in France) and Wild Wood, Part 1.

Aleksandra Michalska
Originally from Poland, Ola moved to Folkestone three years ago. She enjoys being close to the sea and spends her spare time reading about etymology and programming. If she is successful in kicking the cat off the keyboard, she writes about strange things and stranger people.

A L Marchant
A big fan of all things strange, Andy – when he has the chance – runs a bookstall in Folkestone specialising in science fiction. He also runs a playwriting group, The 10 Minutes a Month Playwriting Collective, which can be found on Facebook and Instagram - @10minsamonth.

Andy moved to Folkestone two years ago and greatly enjoys living a twenty-minute walk from the seaside.

Tony Hulse
Born in Folkestone and has lived locally all his life, apart from his university years. He is a teacher of English, Film and Politics and a musician. Tony has always enjoyed writing - songs, short stories, travel pieces. He liked the challenge of creating a ghost story - it was quite an immersive experience - and ended up unsettling himself as he sought to unnerve the reader!

Mark Brophy
After over forty years on planet earth, Mark finally wrote his first book, "The Prince's Parade". It was inspired by the nature of his adopted home of Seabrook near Folkestone which features a unique wild area called Prince's Parade. This remains threatened by housing development and the book has raised substantial funds to fight the legal battle for its protection.

On joining the Write by the Sea group, Mark immediately became involved with the Living Advent Calendar, a yearly creative event in Folkestone for which he wrote his first ghost story, "A Drink with the Dead," included here renamed as "The Thirsty Librarian." He has also written "The Signal-Man of Folkestone Harbour" for this anthology. In his spare time, he drives trains on High Speed One. Mark is also a keen amateur photographer and can often be encountered walking with his Jack Russell, Rosie.

Jana Chatters
Senior Teacher, Czech origin, has lived in the UK for twenty-four years. Enjoys gardening, country walks, Tai chi and swimming, creating mosaics and painting pebbles, as well as writing fiction. In her writing, Jana focuses on the life stories of English people and of Czech people who have settled in the UK, and the problems they have had in adapting. She has written books in both English and in Czech, including Goodbye Comrades (the story of how and why Jana came to England,) and Fall, so you can dance! (stories about three Czech families who came to live in England.)

Paul W Robinson
Began writing children's stories in 2015 after forty years as a teacher and educational adviser. One of Paul's main characters is Charlotte Holmes, a profoundly deaf teenage detective. Paul was very proud recently to have been invited to join a select group of authors, when he was commissioned to write a Lucy Wilson novel. He writes children's crime and science fiction...and wrote Hilary and Nigel RIP, the adult ghost story in this anthology.

Chani Barnes
Comes from New Romney and is 17 years old. Writing poetry is a big part of Chain's life and she loves how it allows her to express how she feels. She struggles with dyslexia and finds it hard to talk to people sometimes, but poetry allows her the freedom to write what she likes and to get out whatever she wants to say. She's fond of music too; she plays the saxophone and the ukulele and enjoys writing music for the same reason as poetry.

Tony Quarrington
Born in Rochester and spent many childhood holidays in Folkestone during the sixties and early seventies. Tony moved to the town in 2016.

He is the co-author of A Half-Forgotten Triumph, a book celebrating Kent County Cricket Club winning their fourth County Championship in eight years in 1913. It was nominated for both the MCC and Wisden Cricket Books of the year in 2013. He plans to publish a book of poetry inspired by Folkestone over the next twelve months and is working on a history of the Old High Street.

Tony has given several readings in local coffee houses, and his literary Zoom meetings during lockdown (and beyond) have been well received. His walking tours of the area are extremely popular and resulted in his receiving the Best Home-Based Business in Folkestone Award in 2019. He currently offers nine different tours.

Margaret Harland-Suddes
Put together and performed, with Mary Leadbetter below, No Known Grave or The Bells of St Eanswythe at the Living Advent Calendar – for Write by the Sea – in 2019. Margaret's most recent novel, Psychopython, published under the name Madeleine Frobisher, was published in 2018. Margaret is currently working on another novel, The Seal Woman, set in Southern

Ireland, and she has recorded and dramatised other work, available on www.audioarcadia.com.

Mary Leadbetter

Local Spiritual Writer and platform medium, serving several Spiritual churches in the area. Her recently published book, "Reach Out to Spirit," contains some of Mary's channelled writing. Mary is also a poet and has put together a compilation of some of her favourite poems, under the title "Feelings into words." The booklet costs £3 and proceeds are given to the Folkestone Rainbow Centre, a charity which helps vulnerable people in the Shepway district. Mary has worked extensively with prisoners and vulnerable youngsters and is a member of the Kent International Healers Association. She is Chairman of the Marsh Ink Writers' Group and has recorded her poetry and short stories for Channel Radio. Contact her on mc_leadbetter@yahoo.co.uk.

Nicholas Irwin

Grew up in Folkestone and went to the Harvey Grammar School. He graduated in Geology from the University of London but inadvertently ended up as a financial auditor. Nicholas retired in 2011 and began to write novels, short stories and poems. Much of his work is of a semi-autobiographical nature, and The Fossil Hunter is an example of that genre. He lives in Ely, Cambridgeshire

Suzannah Gisby

Lives in Dover and works in a mini-supermarket; married to Shaun for thirteen years. Suzannah writes poetry, short stories and plays and has performed some of her poems at Open Mic nights. Took part in the Living Advent Calendar performance with Write by the Sea in 2019, breathing vivid life into the character of Alfred in Words of Comfort.

Printed in Great Britain
by Amazon

71299391R00079